KRISTY K. SCHNABEL

Willful Obsession

A Lake Waluga Cozy Mystery Novella

STAR RUBY

PUBLISHING

To Larry
My love, my light, my rock.

The true mystery of the world is the visible, not the invisible.

—Oscar Wilde

Acknowledgments

Thank you to my ...

- encouraging writing teacher, Johnny Zackel
- helpful and honest Beta Readers: Rachel Bucci, MK Frank, Jennifer Karkanen, Srianthi Perera, Vicki Perris, and Maggie Prevish
- band of encouraging fellow writers and friends
- patient editor, Jen Boles
- meticulous proofreader, Beth Attwood
- talented book cover designer, Donna Rogers
- indefatigable husband, Larry Schnabel, who read my story again and again without complaint

Chapter 1

January 29, 2024

The clicking of Denise Williams's nails on her keyboard halted when her body slumped, slipping her being and legacy into jeopardy. Dawn had broken at 7:04 on this chilly morning in Lake Waluga, Oregon. Denise's longtime cleaning woman, Cora, would arrive at 7:30.

Chompers, Denise's golden Labrador, slept peacefully on his dog bed near her desk. The only light in the room, the desktop's screen, faded to black. Denise's oversize mug with coffee and soy milk grew cool. Her gray-blond hair peeked out of her hand-knit, multicolored wool hat. That and her hoodie, jeans, and socks, which matched her hat, would keep her warm. Denise looked younger than her sixty-five years because she kept physically active, especially with a dog needing frequent walks.

As rain tapped on the skylights, a car's headlights lit up the driveway. Chompers raised his head, unaware of his incapacitated guardian. He walked toward the front door of the tidy, welcoming cottage and wagged his tail, anticipating the knock.

* * *

At seven-thirty a.m., Cora tapped on the Dutch door window, and Chompers responded with an eager bark. Cora tried the knob, which wouldn't turn. Next, she rang the doorbell and cupped her hand against the glass, looking inside. Finally, she located her key and let herself in, singing out "Hello" as she leaned down to pet Chompers.

The tall, sturdy woman in her late thirties effortlessly lifted the cleaning caddy with one hand while toting a vacuum cleaner with the other. "Where's your momma, Chomps?" The dog wiggled and wagged. Cora placed her coat and handbag on the hooks near the front door as she had for ten years. "Denise?"

Cora started toward the kitchen but paused when Chompers ambled to the dining room office. She dropped her supplies when she saw Denise in her chair, unmoving, with her head on her chest. Cora hesitated, and then raced to Denise's side. Cora first nudged her and said her name. She traced Denise's cheek with her fingertips, noting the coolness.

Cora ran to her phone in her purse and called 9-1-1.

"9-1-1, what's your emergency?"

"I found my client collapsed. Please, send an ambulance, quick!" Cora ran back to Denise as she spoke.

"Address?"

"706 Fourth Street, Lake Waluga." Cora made a gasping sound as if she had forgotten to breathe.

"They're on their way. The fire station is close by. Take a deep breath. What's your name?"

"Cora Gabriel."

"Cora, is your friend conscious?"

"No."

2

"Is there a pulse?"

Cora placed two fingers on the inside of Denise's wrist and felt a slight pulse. "A faint one."

"What's her name and age?"

"Denise Williams. Like, early sixties, I think. Oh, I hear a loud truck. I see flashing red lights. They're here!"

"Good. Stay on the line till they come out of the truck."

* * *

Next door, Mary Coleman drank coffee at the breakfast table. Soon, she would leave for her job as director of the city's Parks Department. A tight ponytail held back her shoulder-length salt-and-pepper hair. As she took a bite of her toasted bagel topped with avocado, her husband, Ned, strolled in.

Ned Coleman recently retired as an accounting manager and hadn't yet adjusted to his unstructured lifestyle. His plaid robe fit snugly around his paunch. His favorite morning routine involved relishing the newspaper. At the beginning of the year, *The Oregon Chronicle* reduced its delivery pattern to Wednesdays, Fridays, and weekends. Unfortunately for Ned, today was Monday. He joined Mary at the table with his coffee. "I sure miss getting the paper every morning."

"You don't say?" Mary heard this complaint every non-delivery day. She lately found Ned clingy and adrift.

"Said that before, have I?" Ned asked with a smirk.

Mary rolled her eyes, yet admired that he could laugh at himself. "Remember that Cora comes today at one o'clock. Maybe you can go for a walk or head to the library to stay out of her way?"

"Noted." Ned fiddled with the power cord of his tablet.

3

Mary grabbed her coat, purse, and laptop bag to leave, but the view outside the front window changed. The green and brown palette of trees and shrubbery became uncharacteristically red. A fire truck with lights flashing parked in front of their house and driveway.

"Oh, no. Look! I'm going to find out what's happening."

Ned abandoned his tablet at the kitchen table, stood staring out the window, and watched the fire truck crew move around with deliberate purpose. He heard the door slam as Mary bolted.

* * *

Tall and slender, Mary slipped through Denise's front door ahead of the gurney. She spotted Cora trying to manage the rambunctious Chompers on a leash. Two EMTs worked on Denise, lying on the floor of her office.

"What happened, Cora?" Mary's heart sank as she gaped at the spectacle.

"I found her collapsed ... in her chair when I came in this morning. I called 9-1-1 right away." Cora's voice cracked.

"No. It's too soon. Not yet," Mary said. Her hand rose to cover her mouth. Glancing at Cora, she said, "You're shaking." Mary grabbed her hand to reassure her.

"I was so scared when I found her. I thought she might be ... you know."

"I'm so grateful you were here." Mary tightened her grasp on Cora's hand.

Mary and Cora waited and watched as EMTs attended to their small, frail friend. Mary balanced her concern and curiosity with staying out of the way.

The police arrived, and a small crowd gathered outside despite

4

the cold and rain. In the Lakeview neighborhood, families stayed for decades, so everyone knew each other. Burly Officer Joe Paulson approached the women with his leather belt and holster that creaked with each step.

Joe extended his hand toward Mary, whom he knew through work. "Mary."

They shook hands.

"Joe," Mary said in a quiet voice. "Meet Cora Gabriel. She found Denise when she came to work this morning."

Cora nodded and shook Joe's extended hand. Their eyes aligned and met briefly, as Joe, too, was tall. Her gaze dropped, and she shrunk back, as if hoping to become one with the wall.

Turning to Cora, Joe said, "It must have been a shock. I hate to ask, but would you mind answering a few questions? I need to write up a report. How about we sit down in the kitchen? Denise is in excellent hands."

"Okay," Cora said as she glanced down at Chompers straining on the leash as Joe petted him. She handed the leash to Mary and followed Joe into the kitchen.

As Mary comforted Chompers to calm him and herself down, she listened. She overheard words like "weak pulse" and "BP eighty over fifty." She didn't know how dire the situation was, but she breathed a sigh of relief. Denise was alive. But she didn't regain consciousness, which sent Mary to the bathroom with Chompers to grab a box of tissues. As she wiped her tears and blew her nose, she grappled with the potential loss of her longtime friend.

It seemed like yesterday when Mary and Ned moved in next door to Denise nearly thirty years ago. Denise welcomed them with lemon bars and offered them assistance as they acclimated to the established neighborhood. The two women became fast friends and socialized at summer barbecues and holiday parties. Through the years, they took turns hosting book clubs, knitting circles, and watching over each other's homes.

Denise supported Mary early in her marriage to Ned when she had miscarried. Denise's kindness she would never forget. Complicating Mary's loss was the unresolved grief from a child she gave up for adoption while attending college. Denise helped Mary dispel the myth that the miscarriage was punishment for giving up her child.

Mary snapped out of her reverie when Cora emerged from the kitchen, with Joe close behind. Cora returned to Mary's side as the EMTs pushed Denise's gurney out the front door. One technician looked over at them, but his face revealed nothing. Mary and Cora grabbed hands and held tight as the ambulance took Denise away. Chompers jumped up and down and barked nonstop as he saw his important person leave the house without him.

"This is awful. You can't possibly work today after all this. I'll make sure you get paid for today when you come next week, okay?" Mary asked.

"Thank you. That's so nice. What about Chompers?" Cora's eyebrows shot up, and her face said, *I'm not taking him.*

In her job, Mary frequently had to make big decisions on the fly. She responded, "Ned will not like this, but we'll take care of him for now and then figure something out. Why don't you go? Of course, we won't expect you this afternoon."

As Cora gathered her things, she dropped her keys on the floor, not once, but twice.

Mary said, "You take care now. I'll get my key from home and then lock everything up. I'll leave for the hospital soon and let you know if I learn anything."

Cora left. Mary walked home to tell Ned the news.

* * *

"Is it Denise?" Ned asked as Mary entered their home.

Mary nodded.

Ned outstretched his arms to offer his wife a hug, and they held each other.

"She's hanging on. I've got to get to the hospital." Mary bit her lip.

"But I thought she looked fine yesterday. I talked to her at the mailbox for quite some time, and she seemed okay. I know she has cancer, but—"

"But it's way too soon. The doctor gave her five years less than two years ago. We don't know what's happened. Until we do, I have a favor to ask of you."

"Of course," Ned said. "Anything." He combed the nonexistent hairs on his scalp with his hand.

"Will you take care of Chompers? I know you're not really a dog person, but this is an emergency." Mary knew it was a big ask.

"Sure, I'll do my best. Anything to help Denise."

"Good, thanks. Let's go get Chompers and his stuff, and I'll lock up her house." Mary reached into the kitchen drawer for Denise's house key.

"Oh, you mean have the dog over here?" Ned asked.

"Yes. Let's go." Mary didn't give him a chance to argue the point.

* * *

When Mary opened Denise's front door, Chompers greeted them with an anxious, fast-wagging tail.

"Ned, why don't you find Chompers's food, bed, leash, and a toy? Meanwhile, I'll do a quick search of the house to make sure everything is secure. Oh, I need to find that folder with all the important info."

"You mean that 'just in case' file? Aren't you jumping the gun, dear?"

"Maybe. But the folder has her Advanced Care Directive, too. You're right. I need to remain hopeful. Let's focus on getting the dog settled for now."

They brought Chompers and his belongings to their house. In no time, he sniffed each room. Mary hoped that his occasional wag showed that he'd picked up Denise's scent here and there.

"Do you have any questions about caring for Chompers while I'm away at the hospital? I might be a while."

"I don't know. Do you have suggestions?"

"How about taking him for a walk? Be sure to bring plastic bags for picking up ... you know."

Ned nodded.

"Pop across the street and get advice from Sam and Alex if you need to. They're dog people."

Mary texted her assistant to make her aware of the personal emergency. Before long, Mary arrived at the town's hospital to learn Denise's condition. She knew she could find out more in person than on the phone.

Chapter 2

January 29, 2024

At Community Hospital, Mary determined Denise was in the ER. She approached the reception desk.

"Can you tell me about Denise Williams's status?"

"How are you related to the patient?" the woman asked, simultaneously pulling off an air of friendliness and sternness.

"I'm her best friend and neighbor, Mary Coleman, and I was with her this morning when the ambulance came. Here's my ID." She flashed her city badge to gain favor. Almost everyone in the community knew her name, and most knew her face. She was in no mood to be trifled with.

"If you'll have a seat, I'll have the doctor come speak to you." The unmoved receptionist pointed to the waiting room.

"Can't I see her?" Mary was unsure where to look, as the woman had a lazy eye.

"If you'll have a seat, I'll have the doctor come speak to you," the woman repeated.

Mary wasn't good at waiting. She hated hospitals—the smell, the colors, and the sterility. She crossed her legs, her foot swinging. In about twenty minutes, a doctor approached.

"Mary Coleman?" A short Asian woman with glasses and a white coat approached with her hands in her pockets.

Mary didn't extend her hand. "Yes." She stood and stared at her face, trying to read her.

"I'm Dr. Lucy Tanaka. I'm afraid Denise didn't make it. I'm so sorry. We did everything we could to save her." She paused to let that sink in.

Mary's hand shot up to cover her mouth. She took a seat. After taking a deep breath, Mary spoke. "She had non-treatable cancer. Her oncologist gave her five years. It hasn't been two yet, and she appeared fine. Is that what killed her?"

"It was probably a factor. Prognoses are more art than science. Sometimes cancers spread rapidly under the radar. But today, her heart stopped. Only an autopsy can determine the exact cause of death. The medical examiner, her primary care physician, and her family will decide whether it's necessary. Does she have family?"

"Only a nephew. They aren't close." Mary hesitated. "He may be in prison." Her hand cradled her face.

The doctor pressed her lips and nodded.

"May I see her? I'd like to say goodbye."

"Come with me. Prepare yourself. We work hard on patients to revive them."

* * *

Oh, my darling friend. I can't believe you're gone. Mary sat by her bedside and gazed upon Denise's face. "You weren't supposed to leave us so soon, my dear one. You've left a hole in my heart.

"I'll be forever grateful for all the guidance you gave me

through the years. Most of all, you helped me get through my personal losses. Now, I'll have to get over you without you to help me," Mary said softly to her departed friend.

"I'll do my best by you to fulfill your wishes. Farewell, my friend." Mary kissed her hand and then mopped up her tears with her soggy tissue.

After visiting the nurses' desk and receiving a barrage of questions she couldn't answer, Mary gave them her contact information and promised to get back to them when she knew more.

* * *

When Mary arrived home, she found Ned and Chompers napping on the sofa. Her smile converted to a scrunched nose upon seeing a damp, fur-covered towel on the floor. Although she wished to join them in peaceful slumber, duty called her to find the important folder in Denise's office. Denise had entrusted Mary to be her executor, and she wanted to get to work right away. From experience, she knew keeping busy helped her cope with grief.

Mary recalled the day when Denise shared she'd been working on her will. Mary resisted the conversation, wanting to believe Denise was cancer-free. Pressing the point, Denise explained that mostly everything was going to charities and asked if she would agree to be her personal representative. Mary agreed in order to change the subject, but now her assignment weighed her down.

As Mary entered her friend's home, the cold and stillness enveloped her. *I miss you so much already, dear friend.* She pushed aside her sentimentality and forged ahead to Denise's office.

Images of the morning's tragic event invaded her mind. Denise lying on the floor. EMTs working on her. She shook her head and blinked hard, as if to banish the thoughts.

Mary knew where the will file resided: on Denise's desk, in the first slot of the tiered wire file organizer. And there the folder was, as it should be. Behind it were folders representing Denise's lost dreams: her plans to visit Spain, notes on an article she was writing about overcoming PTSD, cheat sheets for her Spanish class, and details for a watercolor art class she'd enrolled in for spring term.

Mary tilted her head up to prevent the tears from spilling out. As she brought her head back down, Denise's hand-drawn pie chart on the wall, secured with a pushpin, came into view. When Denise got her cancer diagnosis, she focused on her charities. Her pie chart had four slices: reading, housing, hunger, and gardening.

Reading represented the child reading program for which Denise volunteered. Housing meant her hope for more low-income homes for the homeless. Hunger depicted how she valued the Oregon food banks. Gardening was a passion most in the community shared. It was the common thread that pulled everyone together. Most Lake Walugans either had a home garden or a plot in the Community Garden, where people congregated and connected.

As the Parks director, the Community Garden was under Mary's purview. She worked closely with its director, Blake James, and knew and supported his bold expansion plans. The city had set aside the land, but Blake's nonprofit needed to procure the development funding. Although Mary didn't know the exact contents of Denise's will, from their general discussions, she suspected charities on her pie chart would be well-represented.

Mary grabbed the will folder and examined the contents. List of people to call? Check. Advanced Care Directive? No longer necessary. Cremation service contract? Check.

Where's the will?

Mary leafed through all the pages again and again. She kept asking herself where the will could be. She had laid eyes on it before when Denise showed her the folder's location.

It has to be here somewhere.

And so the search began. First, Mary combed through the folders on the desk. Next, she thumbed through the file cabinet. While doing a quick search, Mary found what the hospital needed. She grew weary. Mary prioritized her most pressing tasks on a notepad.

1. *Contact the hospital*
2. *Call Pastor Nelson. Get memorial service date and time*
3. *Notify the contact list*
4. *FIND THE WILL*

Without the will, Mary's fondest, secret dream couldn't come true. She rebuked herself for such a thought at this moment and went home to share the sad news with Ned.

* * *

"There you are," Ned said, rising from the couch as Mary opened their front door. "Any update on Denise?"

"I'm afraid we've lost her." Mary reached for Ned's hands and held them as she explained what had occurred at the hospital.

"I'm so sorry, dear. Poor Denise. Poor you. You must be

wrung out. How are you doing?"

Chompers nuzzled for attention, and Mary dropped to his level to give him some love. "It's been quite a day. I found you two asleep on the couch when I came home, so I went to Denise's to rifle through paperwork."

"You don't have to do that today, of all days." Ned's head slid toward his shoulder.

"I know. Just trying to keep busy. I found the hospital stuff but couldn't find the will."

"Tomorrow's another day. We'll find it. Let's build a fire, order some food, and settle in. Okay?"

"That sounds good. Uh, wait. Darn. I have to call Cora to see how she's doing and break the news. Since you mentioned ordering food, how 'bout Thai? Our usual stuff. The menu with the phone number is next to the coffee maker, okay?"

Ned walked toward the menu.

"I'll join you in a bit," Mary said.

Mary walked down the hall to their bedroom and lay down, releasing a long sigh. She called Cora, and after revealing that Denise had passed, Mary asked how Cora was bearing up after the morning's events.

"Okay, I guess. It's a lot to take in."

Mary pressed her ear to the phone to hear Cora's soft voice. Unassured of Cora's well-being, Mary asked if her husband was around to support her.

After a long pause, Cora said, "I guess I never told you. But Denise knew, so I thought she told you. He left a couple of years ago."

Mary's mouth dropped as she vacillated between doubting her memory and feeling hurt. Although they'd known each other for a long time, since Mary worked, their communications consisted of sticky notes left for each other on the kitchen counter.

"Oh, I'm so sorry, Cora. I had no idea."

"It's for the best. We weren't getting along."

Normally, Mary would delve deeper into such a revelation and offer more sympathy, but not today. "Well, you take care, Cora."

"You, too. See you next week."

Mary stared at the ceiling, depleted. She closed her eyes, and exhaustion overtook her, and she fell asleep. Later, Ned nudged her and led her to the dinner table, which had hot food and enticing smells.

Chapter 3

January 30, 2024

The morning after Denise's death, Mary typed intently on her computer in her home office. Ned came up behind her and rubbed her shoulders. She tilted her head back as she chewed on the top of the pen in her mouth and said, "Thank you."

"What are you working on?" Ned asked, with Chompers wagging his tail nearby.

"I'm emailing documents to the hospital. Lots of paperwork. They asked for next of kin information, so we may have Wayne descending on us. That is, if he isn't in jail."

"If he shows up. Hey, it's chilly in here. Aren't you cold?" The bedroom turned office was situated on the north side of the house.

"No. I'm too busy to think about creature comforts." Mary petted Chompers as he wiggled by. "I'll be meeting with the pastor today to plan the order of service for Saturday. And I have a bunch of calls to make." Mary held up Denise's long list of friends and colleagues.

Ned moved around her chair to gaze at his attractive wife. "How can I help?" He gently pulled the pen from her mouth and handed it to her. "You look tired, dear. You always take on too much. I'm here and willing."

Chompers put his head in the paper recycling bin, grabbed a mouthful, and chewed. Ned redirected him.

"I've come up with a few ideas, actually. Number one, taking care of Chompers is huge—thank you. Two, here are the memorial service details." She handed him her notes. "Do you think you can get this information to the neighbors? They'll want to know what's going on."

Ned rubbed his head as he scanned Mary's notes.

"You can be the biggest help tomorrow. We need to turn Denise's house upside down to find the will and determine her legal and financial profile, bills due, etc. I'm bringing you out of retirement," Mary said as she smiled. "Your accounting skills will be invaluable."

"I accept." Ned grinned and saluted. "I'll need to cancel my pickleball game, but my partner will understand."

"Great. Thanks. Now ... I have some difficult calls to make." Mary started to turn her chair back toward her desk. "Oh, speaking of calls, I forgot to tell you something last night."

"Oh?"

"Cora's no longer with her husband." Mary stared at Ned to see if he knew.

"Really?"

"She said they didn't get along, and he left a couple years ago."

"How 'bout that?"

"I know, right?" Mary paused and cupped her hand on her face. "A few years back, I was at home on a holiday Monday. I

17

spotted a bruise on Cora's shoulder because she wore a tank top on that hot day. I'm ashamed to say I didn't ask her about it."

Ned shrugged. "Water under the bridge, Mary."

"I guess you're right." Mary spun her chair toward her pile of papers.

Ned departed. Moments later, the furnace kicked on, and Ned's loving attention cheered her. Then, she heard him talking to his female pickleball partner. Laughter ensued. *What could they be laughing about?* Mary picked up her pen and bit it.

Only one name had a star next to it on Denise's contact list: Peter Morgan. Although Mary and Denise had been close, Denise became evasive every time Peter came up, and Mary didn't pry. She had empathy regarding closely held secrets.

Mary knew Peter was much younger than Denise. Over the decades, Mary had observed Peter visiting in his old-style Volkswagen van, the kind that hippies and surfers loved. By her estimation, Peter visited about once a month. Denise called him her computer guru for all the tech stuff in the home, but Mary remained unconvinced that Denise needed tech support that often.

One year, Mary saw Peter's photo in the *Lake Waluga Gazette*. He appeared well-groomed and professional, the owner of a successful high-tech company. Mary thought of Peter as two people: a hippie and a computer nerd. Denise kept their relationship elusive, like a hazelnut locked in a shell.

Mary called Peter's number.

"Hello?" Peter asked.

"Ah, yes. Thanks for picking up. This is Denise's neighbor, Mary. We've seen each other through the years."

"Uh ... of course." Peter paused. "Hi, Mary. What's up?"

"I'm afraid I have some bad news." Mary heard a door

slamming shut on Peter's end and surmised he needed privacy at the office. "I'm sorry to tell you we lost Denise yesterday. She died in her sleep." Mary figured a little white lie would be kind. "I'm so sorry."

The line grew silent. Mary heard a choked sob. Hearing Peter's pain put her in touch with her own. She swallowed hard and questioned her ability to speak.

After a deep breath, Peter uttered, "Thanks for letting me know."

Mary quelled her emotions. "Again, I'm so sorry. I'll text you the link to the service details on the church website when it gets posted. It's this Saturday. Maybe I'll see you there?"

"Definitely. Thank you." The line went dead.

After that call, Mary stepped outside to the patio courtyard. The daffodils bloomed, and the tulips were emerging from the ground. She immediately got cold, but didn't care. The briskness helped calm her. Delivering painful news was not her forte. She needed consoling, and yet she was helping soothe others.

Denise had been a social worker for her entire career, and Mary didn't know how she did it. Even after retirement, Denise still worked in the field by publishing articles on her PTSD specialty.

Where's my Denise to help me through this trauma now?

She raised her hands to her cheeks, tapped them lightly to bolster herself, and went back inside for the next challenging call.

Mary didn't know Denise's nephew, Wayne Smithson, well. When Denise's brother died in a drunk driver incident years ago, Wayne came to live with Denise. His mother had disappeared when Wayne was young.

When Denise took him in as a teenager, Wayne struggled with

the loss of his father and acted out. He frequently got in trouble at school related to smoking, drugs, and fights. His behavior distressed Denise, a well-respected counselor. The summer after Wayne's junior year, he turned eighteen, passed the GED test, and took off. Witnessing Denise's distress over Wayne, Mary grew to resent him.

Besides disliking Wayne for how he behaved when Denise cared for him, Mary had a personal reason for despising him. Once, after revealing to Denise he had broken curfew, the following day, Mary found her garden gnome smashed to smithereens. She never doubted that Wayne did it. Her grandmother had given them the irreplaceable family heirloom as a wedding shower gift. Mary admittedly held grudges, and she couldn't forgive his retaliation, even if he had a difficult past.

Reluctantly, she called Wayne's number from the contact sheet, half expecting the call to not go through.

"This is Wayne. Leave a message."

"Hello, Wayne. This is your aunt's neighbor, Mary." As she spoke the words to voicemail, a call came in, and she recognized the area code as the number she had called. She picked up the incoming line.

"Hello?" Mary asked.

"Yep, Wayne here. You rang?"

"Hello, Wayne. This is your aunt's neighbor, Mary." Her voice quavered.

"You're calling about my aunt Denise? The hospital already called."

"So you know. I'm sorry for your loss." Mary wished her words were less robotic.

"Aunt Denise told me years ago you'd handle her will."

"Yes."

"Well?"

"Well, what?"

"Did she leave me anything?" Wayne asked flatly.

The question stunned Mary, leaving her speechless for a moment. "I don't know. We're focusing on the memorial service right now."

"Oh, when's that?"

"Saturday."

"I can be there."

Last Mary heard from Denise, Wayne was in a Nevada prison. Now, she knew he was out, probably on probation.

"Will you be reading the will after the service?" he asked.

Mary once again debated how to respond. She recalled Denise sharing that Wayne lacked the ability to feel empathy. *He just wants his aunt's money.*

"No. Our focus will be entirely on celebrating your aunt's life. I'll text the link to the service info. Goodbye." She regretted hanging up on him, but rationalized it by telling herself it was for her own self-care.

Mary had four days to find the will before the service. She wanted to tell Wayne that Denise had left him nothing. *Am I being too mean? Should I feel sorry for him for having a tough life?* Mary hoped he wouldn't show up.

Chapter 4

February 3, 2024

On the Saturday of the memorial service, the Colemans left Chompers alone in the house for the first time. Anticipating difficulty, Ned tired the dog with a long walk. Besides mourning the loss of his primary caretaker, Chompers suffered from separation anxiety. They knew this from when they helped Denise with her cancer treatments.

Mary and Ned arrived early at the First Unitarian Church of Lake Waluga. Mary noticed a motorcycle in the parking lot and wondered if it belonged to Wayne. Denise had mentioned his affinity for them. She spotted Pastor John Nelson, and the prior thought dissipated.

"Thank you so much, Pastor John, for helping me put this memorial service together so quickly."

"Happy to do it, Mary. Great to see you, Ned."

They gave each other tight-lipped smiles, reflecting the solemnity of the occasion, and then shook hands. Pastor John handed Mary a copy of the printed program.

"Oh, my!" Mary gazed at the photo she'd selected of Denise

and the bio she'd written. "It's lovely." Seeing the finished product in print made Denise's passing real for Mary, and she grabbed around in her purse for a tissue.

Turning to Ned, she said, "Look, didn't ... didn't this ... come out beautifully?" She had stifled her grieving for days, but the program triggered her.

"It's wonderful, dear. Shall we sit?" Ned asked.

Beautiful flower arrangements, abundant with roses, filled the sanctuary, their scent creating a fragrant atmosphere. As Alison Krauss's rendition of "I'll Fly Away" played, mourners filed in. Pastor Nelson asked guests to scrunch together in the pews to make room for others.

At the top of the hour, Pastor Nelson welcomed the crowd and began the eulogy. During his speech, an image of Denise's hand-drawn pie chart from her office wall projected on the screen as Nelson spoke of her charities and volunteer work.

Mary wished she could focus, but uneasiness plagued her as she wondered about Wayne's presence. Ned elbowed her when she kept turning her head to glance behind her, but not before she spotted Peter in the back.

Mary's turn in the program arrived, and she approached the podium. "I still can't believe my best friend and longtime neighbor is gone. I'd like to share a story about Denise and the Community Garden. She had a green thumb with her Double Delight roses, but some of you might not know of her vexations with tomatoes.

"Denise loved homegrown tomatoes, big, fat, juicy ones. Blake James at the Community Garden can attest that she never achieved growing them to her ideal. But she tried. Year after year."

Blake shouted out, "Amen!"

The congregation snickered.

"Denise envied everyone else's success. She figured they all had a secret weapon, some combination of soil and fertilizer, and no one would tell her the magic formula."

Chuckling rumbled through the audience.

Mary ended her speech with "I invite you all to think of Denise the next time you catch the aroma of a Double Delight rose or dig your teeth into a Willamette Red tomato. I'll miss her dearly."

The audience applauded. Pastor Nelson concluded the service and invited everyone into the adjoining room for a reception.

Mary turned to Ned. "I'm so pleased with the robust attendance. I saw Officer Joe. Did you hear that sob in the back? I think it was Peter. Do you think Wayne is here?"

"It was a good send-off, Mary," Ned said as they walked to the pulpit area.

Mary waved to her neighbors, Sam and Alex, who had brought daffodils from their garden. Curiosity got the best of Mary when she spotted a large, exquisite floral wreath. She searched for a card but couldn't find one. She suspected it was from Peter.

Mary approached Blake from the Community Garden, who stood near Cora. "Hi, Cora. Hi, Blake." Mary hugged them and thanked them for coming. "I didn't mean to interrupt."

"Not at all." Blake flashed a wide grin. "Cora and I were brainstorming what she could plant on her plot this spring. Now's the time to plan."

"Yes," Cora said. "You have me, uh, considering Willamette Reds, Mary."

"I loved that story you shared about Denise. I got a kick out of that," Blake said.

Mary smiled and excused herself to greet others.

Later, on the way to their car after the service, the Colemans held hands. Mary breathed in and exhaled deeply.

"It was great, but I'm glad it's over," Mary said.

"Uh-oh," Ned said.

Wayne sat on his motorcycle ahead of them.

Mary's heart sank. "I can't deal with him now," she said through her teeth.

Wayne smoked a cigarette, waiting. He wore a thick beanie and leather jacket, both black. Gray hair speckled his brown beard.

Wayne stood and approached Mary. She'd forgotten what a large man he was and was thankful to have Ned at her side.

"Mary."

"Hello, Wayne." Disdain exuded from her words.

"You know what I want. When can we meet? Now's good."

"Not for me. I'm exhausted." Mary glanced at Ned, and they walked away.

"You'll have to deal with me sometime." Wayne rolled his motorcycle to follow them.

"Not if you're not in the will." Mary turned and stared directly at Wayne.

"Wait ... You said 'if.' You don't know. You either haven't looked ... unlikely, or you don't have it. You don't have the will. Or maybe you can't find the will! I'm a card player, ya know." He held up his fist, revealing playing card suits tattooed below each knuckle. "I'm good at reading people. You can't bluff me."

"Look, I don't even have the death certificates yet. I'll text you when I know more."

Wayne's eyes averted away from Mary toward a man walking in their direction: Officer Joe. They paused speaking as Joe approached while rain sprinkled around them.

"Hello, Wayne. Condolences," Joe said.

"I'm flattered you remember me," Wayne said flippantly.

"How could I forget? Your junior year in high school was my personal nightmare. Is everything okay here? I sense tension."

"We were just leaving. Thanks, Joe," Ned said as he led Mary toward their car.

"I'll be in touch, Mary," Wayne shouted as the couple marched away.

A chill traveled down Mary's spine.

* * *

In the short car ride home, Ned brought up Wayne. "You let him get to you." Ned glanced Mary's way.

"I know." She gazed out the window at the rhododendron and azalea bushes adorning the cottage gardens, adding greenery to the dreary day.

"Remember, he was a kid when his dad died. Any child would struggle with that."

Mary flashed back to when Denise came over one night years ago. With a puffy red face, she held out her arms, and they hugged. The police had arrested Wayne for assaulting a fellow high school student. Denise felt like a failure as a helping professional, unable to keep her nephew out of trouble despite all her training.

Mary took in a deep breath and sighed. "I can't argue that point, Ned. What I get stuck on is how much pain he caused my friend. He wrecked two years of her life after she took him in. Guilt and worry consumed her when he left. They never got on well since. I find it difficult to forgive him for that. And he's made so many bad choices since, you know, the illegal activities."

"Denise sure got the tough part of parenting, didn't she? And none of the joy," Ned said as he turned on the windshield wipers.

"And now he's so entitled, so arrogant. Can you imagine what would happen if I don't find the will? As her only blood relative, he'll get everything. Denise's house alone is worth over a million. She got it long ago when prices weren't so high, but even so, I never figured out how she could afford it on her salary."

Ned pulled into the garage. As they exited, he said over the roof of the car, "Maybe she inherited it like us."

"Maybe. Ready to face the pooch after his first time alone in the house? Prepare yourself."

Ned entered the kitchen from the garage with trepidation. Although they expected Chompers to greet them at the door, they found him in the corner of the family room, head down, tail wagging nervously.

"How'd you do, boy?" Ned asked. "It's okay. We'll clean up whatever's necessary. I don't want you to be afraid of us."

Chompers approached, cowering, and welcomed being petted. Ned peered around the corner from the kitchen and saw ripped newspapers everywhere. Chompers, living up to his name, had a paper party while they were gone.

"It could have been much worse," Ned said as Mary entered the room.

"Haha. Oh, yes, it could have been worse. How 'bout you and Chompers take a little walk, and I'll clean this up."

"Hey, did it ever occur to you that Chompers might have eaten the will?"

"Hilarious. I'm not amused."

"I'm serious. Look at this! He's a paper-shredding machine. What if Denise left the will on her desk, left Chompers alone,

27

and rip, tear, gobble?"

Mary didn't allow herself the possibility Ned could be right. Instead, she smirked to give Ned credit for the joke.

Using his dog voice, Ned said, "Chompers. Walk time!" The dog wagged his tail and then performed the downward dog yoga pose to indicate his eagerness.

Mary needed the alone time. She tidied the living room and then drew a hot bath.

* * *

When they returned from their walk, Ned and Chompers took a nap. Mary loved how they had bonded. Although her bath relaxed her somewhat, the missing will unsettled her. Her thoughts turned to her brother, Magnus, who grew up in Oregon but settled in California after dropping out of law school. Now, he worked as a private investigator, and she loved bouncing ideas off him. She rang him.

"Hey, Sis. Great to hear from you. How was the service?" Magnus asked.

"It was so special. I think Denise would have liked it. But I'm glad to get the event behind me."

"I'll bet."

"Can I get some advice? I can't find her blasted will. I return to work on Monday. Her nephew, Wayne, is breathing down my neck, hoping he's in it. What am I going to do?"

"Take a breath."

"You're annoying."

"I know."

Mary heard him clicking his tongue, as usual, always three times in a row.

"I need your ideas. Where else can I search for the will? Also, I did a Google search, and I believe I have thirty days to file the will with the Probate Department. Can I get an extension from them? Do you know the legal implications?"

"I have a tough question for you," Magnus said.

"What?"

"Why would Denise hide the will?"

"I don't know ..."

"Did she show you where she kept it?"

"Yes." Mary's lips pulled to the side of her face.

"Well, she wanted you to find it easily. Problem is, it was there for anyone to find."

"What are you saying, Magnus?"

"What if someone stole the will?"

"You're so jaded."

"You'd be cynical, too, if you were in my line of work." He released his breath in three bursts, resembling the sound of a steam engine train.

"First, few people had access to the house. Second, why would someone steal it?"

"Well, ask yourself who benefits from the will disappearing?"

"Wayne! Denise mentioned that he's not in the will. So if it can't be found, he's the sole blood relative, and he gets everything." Her uneasiness about Wayne smacked her between the eyes. Like she believed he destroyed her gnome without proof, Mary knew in her bones that Wayne would steal the will, given the chance.

"Bingo. Now you're thinking. Here are my suggestions. Do one more search of the house, just in case. Look in unusual places like the freezer. Let's rule out all the obvious places, like her lawyer's office and a safe deposit box at the bank."

"Uh-huh."

"Then, ask yourself who has keys to the home. I'm happy to do a background check on anyone you like. Shall we start with Wayne?"

* * *

That night, Mary had a fitful sleep. A nightmare woke her up, which also woke Ned.

"What is it? Did you have a bad dream?" Ned asked.

"Yes. I was interviewing for a promotion, but instead of a panel of three people, I had to do a presentation in front of a full auditorium. I couldn't find my PowerPoint file, so I searched and searched on my laptop. Inexplicably, I had an infant on my hip, and he spat up on my silk blouse. Sweat drenched me. The audience laughed, and I felt humiliated." Mary inhaled deeply and sighed.

"We both know what this is about. It's pretty obvious, right?"

"The will," they said together.

"This project is taking a toll on you, Mary. I don't like all this stress on you." Ned turned on his bedside lamp.

"I have to find it." Mary sat up and adjusted her pillow behind her back.

"Why is it so important to you?" Ned sat up, too.

"You know. The charities. Do you want Wayne as a neighbor?"

"It feels like more than that." Ned glared at his wife. "Maybe you could examine that. Are you sure there isn't another reason this is so vital to you?"

Mary covered her eyes with her hand to reduce the light's glare.

Ned tapped Mary's forearm. "You gave Denise a great send-

30

off. It's not your fault that the will wasn't in the folder. At some point, you'll have to say you've done all you can."

Mary knew Ned was right. "I know ..." She didn't want to talk about it anymore and hoped that by agreeing with him, he would drop his objection.

"Look, I'm going to have to put my foot down. You have your health to consider. We'll search for a few more days, and then that's it." Ned's face turned red.

Ned rarely trotted out the "foot down" comment, so Mary knew he meant business. "Let's try to go back to sleep," she said.

I never want him to know the real reason this means so much to me.

Chapter 5

February 4, 2024

Mary spent Sunday planning her next steps.

1. *Determine if Denise has a safe deposit box.*
2. *See if Denise has a home safe.*
3. *Find the contact information for Denise's attorney, if she has one.*
4. *Check the freezer.*

Mary quickly found Denise's local bank in her paperwork, and conveniently, Mary banked there, too.

Next, Mary searched for a home safe, even peeking behind framed artwork. She chuckled at herself acting as a sleuth starring in an Agatha Christie movie. Admittedly, too much was at stake not to explore every possibility.

The file cabinet's contents didn't reveal a relationship with an attorney. Still, after more snooping, Mary found a business card for a law office.

After searching the freezer, Mary knew Operation Defrost

and Clean Out was in her future, but that could wait since there wasn't a will. Monday was going to be a busy day.

Chapter 6

February 5, 2024

Mary arrived at work at seven in the morning. Fortunately, her assistant had prioritized the most critical items on her desk. Mary returned a few emails and calls. She emailed her boss, the city manager, to let him know she would be back part-time this week. She and Victor had a long, productive relationship, and Mary knew he would understand. By ten-thirty a.m., she was out the door to do her errands.

First, Mary picked up the death certificates. That was easy because the Health Department was in the adjacent building. The certificate held no surprises, indicating that Denise had died of natural causes with the significant condition of cancer.

Second, Mary went to the bank. Mary had an acquaintance with the bank manager. When she presented the death certificate, Mary discovered Denise did not have a safe deposit box. The attorney would be more challenging.

* * *

The receptionist perked up as Mary opened the Larson & Weiss Law Office door. Mary had driven past this office countless times but never noticed it.

"May I help you?" the cheerful woman with purple streaks in her long hair asked.

Man, she is young.

"I don't have an appointment." Mary feigned chagrin. She eyed the office, admiring the brick walls and luxurious couches, and determined the practice did well.

"My friend just died." Mary handed the receptionist a copy of the death certificate. "I haven't been able to find the will, but I found a business card for this law office in her Rolodex."

"Her what?"

Oh, boy. I'm feeling old.

"That's not important. Can you tell me if Denise Williams is a client here?"

"We can't give out client information," the receptionist said with a fake smile as she handed back the death certificate.

"She's dead."

The young woman's face turned the color of her crimson-shaded lipstick, and she glanced down. Her boss's door was open, and he popped out. He walked toward Mary, hand extended.

"Hi, I'm Dave Weiss. May I help?"

She shook the hand of the clean-cut, smiling, and smartly dressed man. "Can you tell me if my deceased friend was your client? I can't find her will, and as you know, I have a limited timeframe before the state laws kick in to overrule her wishes."

"Ahh ... unfortunately, the client-attorney relationship exists beyond the grave. So I can't tell you if someone was a client. I can consider bending the rules if you're a beneficiary in the will.

35

Are you?"

Mary's face heated up. "No, but I'm the executor. I mean, personal representative—I think that's the proper term—of the will."

"A will you can't find."

He'd been eavesdropping.

"Right. Well, I know where it is supposed to be. I did lay my eyes on it once." Mary scrunched her face.

"But I may have some good news for you." Weiss sat on the edge of the receptionist's desk and couldn't see her downturned lips.

"Oh?" Mary asked.

"We don't keep original wills at all. Period. The PLF, the liability fund for the State Bar, discourages the practice."

Mary cocked her head.

"You see, anyone can change their will at any time. Multiple originals create chaos."

"So even if she had been a client, you wouldn't have the original will here." Mary sighed and shifted her weight. Deflated, Mary wondered why he thought not having the original was good news.

"Correct," Dave said.

Mary thought a second, and then said, "Okay ... so maybe it's unlikely that any attorney has the original."

"Most likely not. If you can find a signed copy and locate the witnesses, sometimes that will suffice. I'll add that electronic versions of a will don't pass muster with the Probate Department. Find as much as you can, then we can talk." Dave grinned, acting as if the line on his fishing pole had been tugged.

"By the way," he said, "if a will can't be found, probate assumes the decedent destroyed it."

Mary bristled at that thought. "I'll keep that in mind. Thank you for your time."

"You're welcome." Weiss stood up, grabbed a business card from the desk, and handed it to Mary. "I'll add that once I represented someone in court who was sure a particular person had stolen the original will. Unfortunately, we lost."

He made a sad face Mary found intolerable.

"Good luck! Let me know if I can be of service." Weiss opened the door for Mary as she left the office.

* * *

Arriving home, Mary spotted Cora's Honda Element in Denise's driveway. *That's right, it's Monday—one week after Denise's death.* As Mary approached Denise's front door, she waved to Sam across the street, whose leaf blower whined. Its high-frequency screech drowned out the sound of Mary entering. She discovered Cora at Denise's desk, tapping away at her desktop.

"Cora, what are you doing?" Mary's voice sounded scolding.

Cora leaped out of the chair. "Ah, hi, Mary. I didn't hear you come in," Cora stammered.

"What are you doing?" Mary stood with arms akimbo.

"I figured you ... you needed to get into Denise's computer, but it's password-protected. I was ... was trying to hack in for you." Cora fidgeted.

Mary paused to process what she'd seen and heard.

Is Cora being helpful, or does she have improper intent? Why is she so nervous?

Mary had known Cora for nearly ten years and had no reason to suspect her. But she was one of the very few people with a key. Mary downplayed the incident because if something nefarious was going on, she didn't want to tip off Cora about her suspicions.

"I see. Were you able to figure it out?" Mary asked, changing her demeanor to be less confrontational.

"No, I couldn't get past the password screen, as you see." She backed slowly away from the computer.

"Well, don't you worry about this, okay? If you would, please stick to cleaning the house. I'll write out your checks and leave them on the living room table, okay?"

"Okay. Thanks." Cora's body relaxed.

"I suppose you understand that coming once a week is no longer necessary. I'm thinking once a month will be good for now. Does that work for you?"

"Sure. I'll need to pick up another client, but I have a waiting list."

"Good. I'll see you at our house this afternoon. We'll plan an outing to get out of your hair for part of the time."

Cora was already scurrying away to get back to her chores. "Okay, see you then."

* * *

Back home in her sunroom, Mary lounged on her comfy chair with the ottoman. She glanced at her orchids, which needed tending, but she suppressed that thought and opted to do that later. She concluded that she'd learned a lot. The will wasn't at the bank or the law office. Ruling those out pleased her, as if she had made progress.

Although Mary had known Cora for a long time, Mary conceded that she didn't know her well. After all, Mary hadn't known that Cora's husband had been gone for two years. This knowledge led Mary to recall a prior time when she couldn't find her Christmas brooch, the one her mother had given her. Mary wore the vintage red holly flower pin on her winter coat from Thanksgiving to New Year's. One year, it went missing. It crossed her mind then that Cora could have stolen it since she was the only person to enter their home unsupervised. Then Mary chastised herself for having such an unfounded suspicion and considered the pin could have fallen off her coat. She admitted she would never know what happened.

Reluctantly, along with Denise's nephew, Wayne, Mary now considered Cora a suspect. Something the attorney said gave her pause. The electronic will. *Maybe that was what Cora was after? But why? It makes no sense!*

Peter! Peter is Denise's tech guy. Maybe he can help me get into Denise's computer.

"Hello, Mary," Peter said, immediately picking up her call.

"Hey, Peter. How are you doing?" Mary could hear background noise. He took her call from his car.

"Honestly, I'm having a hard time. Denise and I, well, we knew each other a long time."

"I know the feeling."

"Sorry, of course you do. The service was great, by the way."

"Thanks. I thought it went well. I have a favor to ask for Denise."

"Anything."

"When can you come over? I need help hacking into her desktop."

"I can try. Tomorrow night after work? Say seven?"

"Great. Meet you at Denise's. Thanks."

Chapter 7

Mary entered Denise's house early to turn on the heat and lights. She poked around, trying to find places where the will might be tucked away. She discovered what appeared to be an entrance to the attic in the hallway when the doorbell rang.

Mary peered at Peter as she approached the Dutch door window. He had longish, wavy brown hair and wore stylish glasses. He was tall and slender, with a boyish face. Mary guessed he was in his early forties.

"Come in, Peter. Thanks for coming over."

Peter wiped his feet on the mat. He took off his coat and draped it over the sofa in a relaxed manner.

"Can I get you anything? Water, soda, beer?"

"Nah. I'm good, thanks." He walked straight to Denise's chair and sat down.

She didn't want to reveal that Denise collapsed in that very chair. Mary had shut down the desktop computer after the Cora incident, so Peter turned it on, and the password screen popped up. Wordlessly, he began trying passwords. The first three failed. Then, after the fourth try, he was in.

"Wow. How did you do that?" Mary pulled up a chair and sat beside him.

"Denise had a few favorites through the years. She disregarded my pleas to strengthen them. One of her common passwords was 'Chompers1,' which is not very strong, right? Anyway, let me write this one down for you."

Peter wrote *Chompers2000!* on a piece of paper. Mary wondered what importance the year 2000 had.

"What are you looking for?"

"Several things. Ned will help me by compiling her financial information, some of which will be on the computer. And most importantly, I need an electronic copy of her will."

Peter froze.

"Are you okay, Peter?"

"Why do you need the electronic one? Don't you, um, have the original one?" His previously self-assured voice stammered.

"No, actually. It's missing. Had Denise mentioned editing it or anything like that to you?"

"No. Let me show you another file here."

He sure changed the subject fast.

Peter maneuvered through the apps with rapid precision. "This file in Excel has all her accounts, user IDs, and passwords. This should be helpful to Ned."

"Thanks. That's a goldmine."

"Here's the icon to her will creation program. Give me a sec, and I'll print out the electronic version for you."

Maybe I've judged him wrongly. "I'm going to have a Pepsi. Can I get you one?"

"Sure. Thanks."

He changed his mind.

When she returned from the kitchen, the electronic version of the will lay stapled on the desk next to the computer. Mary handed Peter his drink, put hers down, and flipped through the pages. The first bequest revealed a big surprise.

"She's bequeathing you the house?" Mary's voice pitch rose.

"Is she?" he asked in a forced casual voice, eyes downcast.

"It's right here." Mary handed him the will.

"Huh." He returned the will to her as if it were a hot potato.

"Is that news to you?" Mary's eyebrows jumped up.

"Denise hinted she might do that. I never wanted to believe that she would die." He started to cry.

Mary went for the tissue box she used one week ago—it seemed like yesterday. She handed the box to Peter, who took a tissue and blew his nose.

"There, there, Peter. I know this is hard. Let's get our minds off this. Can you help me do one more thing?" She led the way to the hallway and pointed to the access point. "The only place I haven't searched for the will is in the attic. Would you be willing to poke around up there?"

"Ah, gee, really?" His forehead creases accentuated.

"I want no stone unturned."

"Why would she, like, hide her will?"

"I don't know. I want to be thorough. Could you?"

"All right." He had stopped crying. "I'll get the ladder from the garage. Do you think you could find a flashlight?"

Mary found a flashlight in the kitchen drawer, and Peter brought in the ladder. He was agile, and Mary was glad he would take on this task. He was up there for about ten minutes and then started down the rungs as bits of insulation rained down.

"There's nothing up there."

"I sure appreciate you checking. Thanks."

"No problem. If that's all, like, I need to get going."

"Of course. I'm most grateful."

Peter put the ladder away, grabbed his coat, and was off.

* * *

Back home, Ned and his new buddy had already gone to bed. Mary turned on the family room fireplace, grabbed the comforter, settled into her favorite spot on the couch, and began reading. Most of the will's language was boilerplate, but she didn't want to miss a thing. Although she lacked legal training, she had reviewed many contracts throughout her career. The bequests boiled down to:

1. *The house goes to Peter*
2. *The Oregon kids' reading program: 20 percent*
3. *The homeless housing program: 20 percent*
4. *The food bank consortium: 20 percent*
5. *The Community Garden: 40 percent*

Bless you, Denise! Except for the house, the will reflects your pie chart. Blake's dream can become a reality.

Mary didn't know how much the rest of Denise's estate was worth, especially since she didn't know if Denise had debt. Ned would help figure that all out. Of course, there were taxes to consider, as well. The will's other bonus was that there was no mention of Wayne.

Man, I have to find that original will, or Wayne will get everything. It's only nine-thirty p.m. Magnus would still be up.

"Hiya," Magnus said, answering the call.

"Hey, you got a sec? I want to update you."

"Same. You go first," Magnus said.

"Well, the original signed will is still missing, but I have an electronic version now." She told him about the house and charity breakdown.

"You must be excited about the Garden part, right?" Magnus asked.

"Let's not count our chickens, but Brother, you don't know the half of it. Maybe I'll tell you someday. Moving on, we can rule out all the locations you suggested I check out. I'm coming to your way of thinking about a possible theft."

"Really? Any new suspects?"

Mary told him about the Cora incident.

"Interesting twist ... My turn?"

"Shoot," Mary said.

"They incarcerated Wayne for fraud, embezzlement, and theft in Nevada from the fall of 2018 until November 15, 2023. When did Denise ask you to be her executor?"

"Let's see. It was a few months after her diagnosis when she was getting her affairs in order. She got her cancer diagnosis two years ago, so I became executor during the winter of '22."

"So ... unless you've seen Wayne around in the last few months, I think he's unlikely to be the thief."

"He's hard to miss. I would have seen him or heard his motorcycle, at least."

"Have you been away from home since November?"

"Only at Thanksgiving when we went to Seattle." While Mary cogitated on that, she heard Magnus's tongue clicks.

"If Wayne visited while you were away, about that time, would Denise have told you?"

Mary clenched the top of the pen in her mouth. "Honestly,

I'm not sure. Denise could be secretive, like with the Peter stuff. She knows I can be unforgiving, whereas she would never give up on Wayne. At the same time, Denise didn't enable him either by giving him money that he'd squander by gambling."

"Keep him on the suspect list, then?"

"I think so." Mary thought some more, then added, "There was this moment in the church parking lot when I witnessed him mentally deduce that I didn't have the will. I wonder if he was playing me. Maybe he'd visited his aunt over Thanksgiving and swiped the will then."

"Could be. By the way, since he's on probation, he probably isn't allowed out of the state. Keep that in your back pocket. If he troubles you, call the police, and they'll probably arrest him."

"Good to know. Thanks."

"So you want to add Cora to the list of suspects? I can run a background on her."

"I think so." Mary bit her lip. She hated being so suspicious, but she rationalized that it was for a good cause.

"What about Peter? Why would Denise leave him the house?" Magnus asked.

"It's so strange, isn't it? I don't have their relationship figured out. I can't think of why someone wouldn't want a million-dollar house. He doesn't need the money. He's a tech millionaire, yet he drives this vintage VW van."

"I suggest we run a check on him to be thorough. In the meantime, can you think of a way to learn more about Cora?"

"Hmm ... Actually, I do have an idea there. Okay. Thanks, Magnus. Stay in touch."

Chapter 8

"You what?" Ned asked. The couple's morning coffee conversation turned adversarial.

Mary mistakenly confided in Ned that Magnus had ordered background checks on Wayne, Cora, and Peter.

"This has gone too far, Mary. You're not a detective. I don't like Wayne being in our lives at all. He's a criminal. And if he thinks he might get his hands on a million dollars, we don't know what he's capable of. I fear for your safety." Ned's face reddened.

"I just—"

"Suspecting Cora, who we've known and trusted for years, strains credibility." Ned paced as he gesticulated. "Peter, well, I don't know him. I don't like you mixed up in all of this."

With her fingers pressing against her forehead, Mary said, "Oh, Ned. I'm not afraid of Wayne. I see him as the confused, selfish boy he was at seventeen. I need you to understand that I want to see this through." She stared at Ned. "It's important to me to fulfill my promise to Denise. Plus, I'm trying to get the charities the money she intended. It's a good cause. I need your support, not your unfounded worries."

"But when will this all end?" He tapped his finger on the table.

"On Leap Day. That will be thirty days after Denise's passing. If I don't find the will by then, Wayne will post the death certificate in court and attest that she died intestate, you know, without a will." Mary softened her voice to calm Ned down.

"So, as you can see, love, I have a few weeks to figure this all out. Then, I will begin administering the will or watch helplessly when Wayne moves in next door. I jest because he will probably sell. Bear with me till then?" Mary tilted her head.

"Begrudgingly." Ned got up to get another cup of coffee. Because it was Wednesday, he took the newspapers into the living room. "Come on, boy." Chompers followed.

Chapter 9

February 9, 2024

After Mary's squabble with Ned, she stayed away from the will project for a couple of days. Her progress was stymied until she heard back from Magnus. She poured herself into her professional work that needed attention. Her assistant arranged a brief meeting with her staff to reconnect, support them, and thank them for covering for her.

The moment Mary felt caught up with her work, Wayne called. She let it go to voicemail and then looked at the voicemail transcription via her phone app so she didn't have to hear his voice.

"Hello, Mary. This is Wayne. I wanted you to know that I've been in touch with a friend who knows legal stuff. He suggests I give you till the end of the month. Then I can file the death certificate 'interstate,' meaning my aunt has no will. He thinks I'll get everything. Till then ..."

"That man!" Mary spat out.

* * *

Later, at home, Mary's cell rang. It was Magnus.

Finally!

"Did you find anything out?" Mary walked to the back bedroom so that Ned wouldn't overhear.

"Hello to you, too."

"Sorry. It's been stressful around here. Ned doesn't want me working on the will anymore. A lot is going on at work. And Wayne called."

"Oh, yeah? What did he want?"

"To give me a deadline, or he'll file an 'interstate' death certificate. He said he talked to a friend who knows the law. If he thinks it's called 'interstate' rather than 'intestate,' his friend is no legal eagle." She chuckled at Wayne's malapropism.

"Right. Well, I definitely found some intriguing things." Magnus cleared his throat.

"I'm listening."

"Did you know that Cora's husband is off the grid?"

"They're separated. What do you mean?"

"She filed a missing person's report over two years ago. He's been untraceable since, meaning he has no legit job, cell pings, or credit card charges. These days, it's difficult not to leave a trail. He is out of the country or dead."

"Wow." Mary's thoughts swirled. "I know so little about him, just that his name is Floyd, and he works in construction. Could he be taking money under the table and paying cash for everything?"

"Maybe ... but if he isn't a criminal, why? It's difficult to do these days."

"Uh-huh."

"There's more. Peter is squeaky clean and rich. That van you mentioned is one of several cars he owns. Most of the others are high-end. That van could be a sentimental memento. Did you know he's married? No kids."

"Married. Hmm." Mary sat at her desk and circled her fingers inside a rubber band like a hamster on a wheel.

"Do a Google search, and you'll see pictures of him with his wife. I don't know … She looks like a place-filler to me."

"Meaning?" Mary asked.

"From searching the photos online, my Spidey sense tells me … The couple appears … detached. I wouldn't be surprised if Peter loves that van more than her."

"What do I do now? Any suggestions?"

"If I'm being honest, if I had to bet on this, sorry, if I'm hedging too much … Just thinking in terms of human nature …"

Magnus breathed out a rhythmic puffing like a steam train.

"I hate to say it, Sis, but I think it's most probable Denise wanted to change her will. People often do. Maybe she ripped it up, thinking she would update it, and she didn't get around to it in time."

"Hmm … That's the second time I've heard that." Mary drank in Magnus's words, but they tasted bitter.

"Sorry, that's what I think. But if you want to pursue this, see if you can find out more about Cora and her long-lost husband. In about four years, she can declare him dead. If there's any life insurance, they'll award that then."

"Another piece of the puzzle."

"As for Peter, I don't see anything there except … doesn't it seem strange that Denise gave him the house?"

"Thanks, Magnus. You've given me a lot to think about."

"You bet."

Mary aimed the rubber band at the filing cabinet and let it fly. *Thwack.*

Chapter 10

February 11, 2024

O n Sunday, the Colemans went to church in the morning as usual. Being February, Pastor Nelson's sermon featured Black History Month. Mary and Ned were eager to get home because they were hosting a Super Bowl party later, but Mary paused when she discovered Blake and Cora in the foyer.

"Hi, you two," Mary said, with Ned close by. Guilt-ridden over ordering the background check, Mary stared directly at Blake, avoiding Cora. Ned examined his watch and tapped it to signal Mary they needed to leave.

"Right, we need to get going, but not before I invite you both to our Super Bowl party today. Sorry for the late invite. Come if you can. Blake, I'll text you our address. Two o'clock," Mary said.

Cora gave a noncommittal, forced smile.

As the Colemans headed toward the door, Blake said, "Warning: I'm a Seahawks fan!"

Mary turned toward him and flashed a thumbs-up.

As they walked to the car, Ned asked, "That was unexpected."

"What?" Her tone had an edge to it.

"We've never invited Cora or Blake socially before. They aren't our close friends. Don't you think it'll be awkward with Cora?"

"Maybe … I thought it would be nice to widen our social circle."

"Indeed." Ned pursed his lips sideways.

* * *

Ned brought in extra chairs and a long table for food into the family room, where the largest TV resided. Chompers milled around excitedly, feeding off the anticipatory energy of his caretakers. Neighbors and friends began arriving after two.

The family across the street arrived first. Sam wore her usual baseball cap and today's featured the local women's soccer team, the Portland Thorns. Her wife, Alex, the baker in the family, carried her trademark cheese-stuffed pretzels. Alex's long blond braid swung as she set down the tray. Their gangly teenaged son revealed his shyness at adult parties by slithering in behind Alex to avoid greeting people, snagging one of his mom's pretzels on the way.

Blake entered holding a six-pack of Buoy Beer IPA in his right hand, and his left arm cradled a platter. True to his word, he wore a Seahawks cap and jersey.

Mary greeted him, grabbed the six-pack to put in the fridge, and handed one can back to him. As she peeked under the platter's foil cover, she asked, "Twice-baked potatoes?"

"Crispy stuffed potato skins. They're my mother's special recipe. Mmm-good! I adjusted the recipe to use baconless bits in case we have some vegetarians in the group. I can't tell Momma that since she takes pride in her recipes. She loves to cook, and Dad likes to eat." Blake let loose his delightful chuckle.

"How sweet of you," Mary said. "Our neighbor Sam will appreciate your vegetarian gesture. They look delicious." She busied herself in the kitchen. "Do you think Cora will come?" *Does my anxiety show?*

"I doubt it. She's kinda shy, and I don't think she's a football fan, either."

"Uh-huh. Well, I'm delighted you came. Grab some food and make yourself comfortable. Ned can introduce you around."

Mary and Ned played hosts, making sure everyone had food, a drink, and a seat. Chompers had been sullen of late, probably because of Denise's absence. People brought out his joyfulness, and he enjoyed their petting. To Mary's horror, he put his paws on the food table and grabbed one of Blake's potatoes before anyone could stop him. Ned corralled the dog into the kitchen, but Chompers had already gulped his prize. Those who witnessed the scene laughed. Mary glanced at Blake and shrugged.

"I doubt he'll want another one. They have jalapeño peppers," Blake said with a wince.

"Chompers belonged to Denise. We're still learning how to train him," Mary said.

"Let me know if I can help, Mary. We're veterans with Labs," Sam chimed in.

"Thanks, Sam. We'll eventually rehome him, but we've been preoccupied."

After kenneling Chompers, Ned reentered the room in time to hear the word "rehome," and his face fell. He said nothing.

On the TV, the gigantic American flag covered the playing field, and Reba McEntire sang "The Star-Spangled Banner."

The room quieted, and some placed their hands on their hearts.

When the singer finished, Alex approached Mary. "How are you doing with the loss of Denise?" Alex's head craned toward her shoulder.

Mary put her hand on Alex's arm. "How kind of you to ask. It's been rough. But there's so much to do when someone dies, so that's keeping me busy."

Alex nodded. "Let us know if there's anything we can do."

"Since you mentioned it, I've been meaning to ask you … You work from home still, right?"

"Uh-huh."

"Maybe you can keep an eye on Denise's place during the day when I'm at work."

"When I can, sure. I see her house from my office window. What am I looking for?"

"Anything suspicious." Mary lowered her voice, even though most of the crowd had their eyes glued to the ad on TV. "Denise's nephew, Wayne, is in town, and I don't want him snooping around until we settle her estate."

"You got it." Alex's cheeks rose as she smiled. She tapped Mary's forearm in a reassuring way.

"Kick-off!" Ned yelled to get everyone's attention on the game. Half showed interest, and the rest liked socializing. Mary straddled her time between those visiting in the kitchen and others so entranced by the football, they welcomed drinks being delivered.

The room erupted when the 49ers scored against the Chiefs. Staring at the room, Mary belatedly noticed that nearly everyone wore red, the color of both teams.

"Did you see that play, Blake?" Ned asked.

Blake watched intently. "I love me a trick play."

Mary leaned against the living room wall, arms and legs crossed casually, grinning from ear to ear at the joy in the room. People ate, drank, conversed, and had a good time. She particularly liked Ned and Blake warming to each other. Mary believed Ned could have more friends, although he was a generation older than Blake. Despite her contentment with the success of the party, Mary missed Denise's presence. She concluded she would have to get used to that.

Next to Blake, Sam asked, "What makes that play a trick play?"

"Well, you see, most times, the defense expects the quarterback to either pass or hand off the ball. In this case, the quarterback threw to the receiver. But, instead of running with the ball, the receiver threw the ball across the field. McCaffrey caught it and ran twenty or so yards in for a touchdown."

"That cross-field throw was risky, but it worked," Ned said. He lifted his arm and simulated the throw.

"The defense wasn't ready for that," Blake said with a chuckle.

"I see. Thanks," Sam said.

"Here's the replay," Ned said as he stood and pointed at the TV.

Everyone cheered again except Sam and Alex's son, who wore a Chiefs cap. Instead, he refilled his plate with food. The teenager would have the last laugh, though, when the Chiefs ultimately prevailed.

After the game ended, people departed. Mary handed Blake's empty tray back to him. "Thanks for bringing your delicious potatoes. Let your mom know they were a hit."

"Will do. I'll leave out the part that Chompers got one."

"Yes!" Mary said. "Will you be at the Garden tomorrow? I might drop by." She tilted her body to the right.

"Sure will. Thanks, Mary. This was a great time."

"Good night."

Chapter 11

February 12, 2024

O n the day after the Super Bowl, Mary dropped by Waluga Farm, an area her department managed. The fifty-acre complex included walking trails, a stone labyrinth, a historic farmhouse, a picturesque duck-filled lake, and the Community Garden. She knocked on the Garden's office door.

"Come in," Blake said.

As Mary entered, Blake beamed. "Glad you could make it, Mary. I don't get many visitors this time of year. It's usually so quiet here in the winter." He stood a tall, solid six foot four.

"I'll bet. Good morning."

"Have a seat. Can I get you some coffee?"

"Thanks. Black, please."

Blake prepared the coffee and handed it to Mary as steam rose from the cup. He pulled out his desk chair and sat down, and Mary sat in the adjacent chair. She glanced at his cupholder full of ballpoint pens with the gnawed caps. Invoices, purchase orders, and catalogs littered his desk's surface. She found a spot for her coffee.

"Yesterday was fun. Thanks for inviting me."

"Happy you could come. I should mention that this is an unofficial visit."

"Oh?"

"I'm Denise's personal representative for her will, and in order to do my duty, I've been sleuthing."

"Sleuthing? Sounds mysterious." Blake's eyebrows shot up.

"Yes. I'm hoping you can help me by telling me anything you can about Cora." Mary leaned her body in, placing her arms on Blake's desk.

"Hmm. Can I ask why?"

"It's probably better if you don't."

"Well." Blake tapped his fingers on his mouth. "As you know, she has a plot here and has for years. That's how I know her."

"Have you seen her husband here?"

"Speaking unofficially?" Blake's eyes danced around.

"I wish you would."

"I think she comes to the Garden to escape her husband."

"Why do you say that?"

"A while ago, Floyd showed up here lookin' for her. He acted all belligerent, ya know, obviously feeling no pain. Drunk. I had to get involved because when he found her, he got loud and yelled, creating a disturbance. He got rough, pushing and dragging her around."

Mary scowled. "Oh, my."

"I had to intervene. He woulda swung at me, but, ya know, he saw me and thought the better of it." Blake lowered his head and shook it.

"Thanks for helping Cora, Blake."

"She was crying. Floyd sure seems like the jealous type and

was making all kinds of accusations."

"Horrible. How did the situation end?"

"She gave in to him and went home. Thankfully, she drove."

"When did all this happen?"

"Not last year. The year before, I think, so 'bout two years ago."

About the time Magnus said Cora's husband had gone off the grid.

Mary flashed back to the bruise on Cora's shoulder, and a twinge of guilt surged through her body. "Would you mind showing me Cora's plot?"

"Sure. I'd love to stretch my legs."

Mary placed her half-finished coffee mug in the sink, and they left the office. The outside air chilled her, and she zipped up her jacket. As they walked the pebbled path past the raised beds of vegetable and flower gardens, Mary took advantage of the opportunity to get to know Blake better.

"You mentioned your parents yesterday. Where do they live?"

"Washington. Dad owns a nursery in the Tri-Cities. He'd love to have me back, ya know?"

"I can see that, but we want you to stay, of course." Mary glanced up at Blake, then got distracted by an elaborate scarecrow replete with overalls and a straw hat.

"I am determined to make a go of it here, but as you know, I need to find the funding to expand this place. I'm all about improving things with innovative concepts."

"Uh-huh." Mary tried to act casual, but his words riveted her.

"I'm giving myself two years to get the funding, or I may have to heed my father's wishes and return to the family business. I'd rather stay here and see my ideas get off the drawing board to become a reality."

"Right." Mary's heart lurched, and her head wanted to explode with thoughts and opinions—too many to voice. Instead, she changed the subject. "So, do you have siblings?"

"No, just the three of us." Blake turned his head toward Mary with a closed-mouth smile.

"And are you a close family?" Mary stumbled a little over a hose blocking her path.

Blake grabbed Mary's elbow to steady her.

"We're as close as we can be given how different we are. By the way, Mom's Black and Dad's white. I don't take after either of my parents, actually."

"Uh-huh," Mary said while trying to act nonchalant.

"They're quiet and like to read a lot. I'm big and tall and gregarious." Blake held out his arms to exaggerate his size. "I like to change and make things better, but they like things to stay the same. I'm talking too much." Blake brought his hand to his mouth.

But Mary had zoned out. Blake's earlier words reverberated in her mind: *I don't take after either of my parents.*

Mary suppressed her reaction but allowed her fists to clench and jerk.

Blake stopped and pointed. "We're here. This is her spot."

"Huh?" Mary returned to the moment.

"This is Cora's plot." Being winter, the ground had dead stems and weeds. They stood on the northeast corner of the Community Garden. Directly to the east of Cora's area stood the communal shed, which contained shovels, wheelbarrows, hoes, and other gardening supplies.

Acreage to the east, parallel to the Garden, was the designated expansion area. The city earmarked the property to expand the Garden. Mary skirted around the shed and eyed the unimproved land.

"I do hope you can develop this area ..." Mary said. As she spoke, she surveyed the view and appreciated the beauty of the skyline, even in winter.

"Don't get me started." Blake chuckled. "I keep thinking of new things to add: an irrigation system, a children's garden area, picnic tables for gatherings, and a structure for holding classes on gardening. My ideas are endless."

"Someday," Mary said wistfully, not knowing if she'd successfully find the will. "Thanks so much for your time and for showing me Cora's plot."

"Happy to help."

"It's so beautiful this morning. Waluga Park looks so inviting. I'm going to take a walk on the path and get some exercise. I'll see you later."

"Good to see you, Mary." Blake gave her a wave as he peered at a weed that needed pulling and yanked.

* * *

Although Mary always enjoyed seeing Blake and loved the views on the paved Waluga path, this moment in her life weighed on her. She ticked through the pressures she faced as she walked.

I need to find the will before Leap Day, fulfill Denise's wishes, fend off Wayne, fit work in, keep Ned happy, rehome Chompers, determine Cora's role, and decide whether to involve an attorney.

It's all too much.

Mary's heart pounded. She headed back toward her car near the Community Garden. Suddenly, her world spun and light-headedness caused her to slow her gait.

I wish I had brought some water. I'm probably dehydrated.

Although the temperature was in the forties, Mary perspired, incommensurate with her exertion. Then, a stabbing pain struck her chest.

Oh, my God! Is this a heart attack? I'm only sixty-one.

Still, she pressed on toward her car, toward the Garden, toward Blake, who could help her. She spotted him and waved, not like a hello wave, but a distress signal.

And then she collapsed.

When she came to, Blake leaned over her.

"Mary, I've called an ambulance. You're going to be all right. Just relax. Breathe slowly through your nose. They're on their way."

Mary raised her hand, and Blake grabbed it. She smiled. Her ear held pooled tears, and her body shook.

"I have a blanket in the office. I can be back in a flash."

Mary shook her head. Blake stayed. His being with her gave her solace. *I'm not ready to join Denise. Not yet.*

* * *

Everything was a blur to Mary. She sensed she was in the hospital. Someone had attached an IV to her hand, and it stung if she moved it. A cuff was on her arm, taking her blood pressure every few minutes, creating pain. She was wearing a hospital gown, and stickers and wires were stuck to her chest. A familiar face approached.

What's her name again?

"Hello, Mary. Perhaps you remember me? I'm Dr. Lucy Tanaka. We met recently when you were here for your friend, Denise Williams."

"Yes." Mary's voice sounded older than she wanted.

"I have some good news for you. You didn't have a heart

attack." She let that sink in. "Are you under a lot of stress?"

Mary nodded.

"Well, I'm not surprised. You've had a panic attack. It presents like a heart attack, but your EKG is fine. I've given you a light sedative in your IV. Your husband is on his way. I can release you, but I want you to reduce your stress. Can you promise me that?"

Mary nodded.

"I recommend you find a therapist, someone you can talk to. I'll add some referrals to your discharge papers. Although it's been nice seeing you again, I don't want you back in the hospital. Okay?"

"Thank you, Doctor."

"Take it easy for a few days. You can return to work on Thursday, okay?"

As the doctor ducked behind the curtains, Ned came in. "My Mary." He kissed her on her forehead.

Chapter 12

Back at home from the hospital, Ned hovered over Mary. Although her episode wasn't life-threatening, his obsequiousness revealed his vulnerability, his fear of being alone. Resting wasn't Mary's strong suit. She tried reading and watching movies, but relaxing didn't make her to-do list disappear.

Mary agreed to stay home for two days. Ned made her promise to see a therapist, and she agreed. But she didn't agree to put aside the will project with only two weeks remaining. Sam and Alex learned of her episode and popped over with tulips from their garden. Although embarrassed by the attention, Mary clasped her hands and held them to her chest to have such kind neighbors.

Chompers showed signs his new living arrangement was permanent by staking favorite spots in the Colemans' home. Whenever possible, they diverted him with walks. Today, on a longer walk than usual, Ned returned with a bouquet of roses.

"Happy Valentine's Day, dear." Ned beamed as he entered

the sunroom.

Mary touched her hand to her heart, and her eyes became moist. "Thank you, hon. I don't know why I'm so emotional. You're a dear man." She reached out to kiss him. "These are beautiful. I'm afraid I didn't get you anything this year. Can I make it up to you later?"

"No need. I want you to get through all this so we can return to how things were. I know you've been through the wringer lately."

"Thank you, sweetie." Chompers, sensing the room's mood, bounded over to Mary, and she hugged him, saying, "Who's a good boy?" while he wiggled.

Chapter 13

February 15, 2024

O n Thursday morning, Mary woke early. She would return to work no matter what Ned said. In the shower, lathering shampoo into her scalp, her thoughts coalesced. The missing will, Cora's attempted hack of Denise's computer, Cora's reticence about her missing husband, and his disappearance became connected in Mary's mind.

What if Cora killed her husband? Nah. What a thought! But she had the perfect burial location adjacent to her Garden plot. OMG. What if she took the will because she didn't want the Community Garden to get the funding for the expansion because it would reveal her husband's body? Cora likely knew about the estate plans from the pie chart on Denise's office wall. And she had easy access to the will on the desk. Is this crazy idea possible?

Mary gasped at the audacity of her thoughts and couldn't towel off fast enough. She needed to talk to Officer Joe. The police station was in the same complex as her work. She got ready quickly, wrote a note to Ned, and headed off.

* * *

In her office, Mary texted Joe.

Mary: Hey, Joe. Any chance you can swing by my office today? Here all day.

Joe: I'll try to come by this afternoon. No promises. I don't plan my day ;-)

At about four-thirty, while Mary read contracts in her office, Joe approached. The half-empty office was quiet and dim.

He poked his head in. "Is now okay?"

Mary smiled. "Yes, thanks. Come in, please." She closed the door and pointed to the empty chair. "Joe, this is off the record and confidential. It's personal, not work-related. Well, it may become work-related to you. I don't know." Mary's words spilled out without her usual forethought.

"I'm listening." Joe stared at her mug full of pens with bitten caps, which drew Mary's attention, and she moved the pen holder.

"I'm the personal representative of Denise's will, only it's missing. She left it in a folder, which was where it was supposed to be. The other paperwork was there, but the will vanished. I've been trying to figure out what happened to it, and I have a few suspects."

"Suspects?" His eyes widened. "You mean you think someone stole it?" Joe placed his right ankle on his left knee.

"I do."

"Is Wayne on your list?"

"We haven't eliminated him yet. 'We' includes my brother, Magnus. Did you know he's a PI in California?" Mary's clasped hands rested on her desk.

"Wow, you're serious. What can I do?"

67

"Right now, I'm suspecting Denise's cleaning woman, Cora. You took her statement."

Joe nodded.

"I've discovered that she had a mean husband, probably a substance abuser, who possibly abused her physically, as well." Mary looked at Joe expectantly, hoping he would reveal something like a domestic dispute call, but his face told no tales.

Mary continued, "I'll admit that I saw a strange bruise on her once, and I let it go. Back to her husband. He's been off the grid for two years, according to Magnus. And Cora never mentioned it to me." Mary lowered her voice. "I've known her for a decade. She's at my home once a week. And she never shared that her husband was gone. Strange, right?"

"Well," Joe said, "victims experience many emotions ranging from shame to embarrassment, and sometimes they want privacy."

"Most importantly, she had easy access to the will."

"Where are you going with this, Mary?" Joe rested his chin on his hand.

"I'm just going to blurt this out. What if Cora killed her husband and buried him in the vacant lot next to her plot in the Community Garden?"

Joe's body jerked back as if he'd smelled sour milk. "Whoa, Mary, that's quite an accusation. Quite a leap." Joe put his hands up in the air. "Putting that aside, why would she take the will?"

"Remember the pie chart on the big screen during Denise's service?"

"Vaguely ..."

"Anyway, I've seen the electronic version of the will. Forty percent of Denise's estate, not counting the house, goes to the Community Garden for its planned expansion project. That would require excavating, which would reveal the dead body."

"Holy crap, Mary. You have an imagination."

"Well, you know my next question. Do I have enough to get the police involved? Like looking for her husband's body on the vacant land at the Garden?"

"Not a chance. You have a lot of suspicions, some coincidences, perhaps, but not enough to warrant searches. Citizens have rights, and judges balance those rights with the police's duty to investigate. There isn't enough here." Joe shifted toward the edge of his chair, on the verge of rising.

"Well, I'm disappointed, but not surprised. I'm trying to do everything I can for my friend, to see her last wishes fulfilled."

As Mary said these words, Joe got up.

"I know, Mary. There's only so much you can do. I wish you luck in finding the will." Joe put out his hand, shook Mary's, and left.

Mary considered what to do next when a text pinged her phone.

Wayne: Two more weeks to find the will. Tick tock.

"Dirtbag!" she said aloud.

The text pushed Mary over the edge. As she reached her tipping point, her blood pressure rose. She would never forgive herself if she hadn't overturned every stone. Literally. Time to organize the "Big Dig."

* * *

Mary devised her plan on the drive home. As she turned onto their street, she passed her neighbors' house. As usual, Sam was out in the yard and carried large bags of bark dust. Mary waved.

Mary determined she needed four people, shovels, gloves, outdoor lights, flashlights, and water. She could get the supplies from the Parks Department shed. She had flashlights and water at home. What she needed most were strong and trustworthy helpers who were willing to take part in a dodgy venture. Taking the path of least resistance, Mary walked over to Sam and Alex's house.

Mary knocked on the door. Alex answered as Sam entered from the garage, dusting herself off.

"Hi, Mary."

"Hi, Alex. Do you and Sam have a sec?"

"For you, of course. Come in."

Alex led the way to the living room, her yellow braid swaying on her back. They passed a wall of photos, mostly of their son through the years.

Alex pointed to the chair across from the sofa facing the large windows with a view of the front yard. Tucker, the chocolate Lab, wagged her tail as she greeted Mary, then returned to her dog bed near the woodstove. Sam sat next to Alex on the sofa.

Mary shifted in her seat, unsure how she'd approach the Big Dig topic. "How's your son doing?"

"Great. Did you know he has a job at our local Subway? He's taking college courses and putting money aside. All good," Sam said.

"Glad to hear it," Mary said.

"We're so grateful for that favor you did for us, not turning him in for that incident at the park."

"Say nothing of that. You're wonderful parents, and he's a good kid. He needed a push in the right direction. Look, I have a bit of a crazy idea to suggest. Better yet, let's call it an adventure." Mary leaned forward with her hands clasped between her knees.

Sam leaned back, extending her arm on the back of the sofa to pet their cat, who had come to investigate.

Alex mirrored Mary's body posture and leaned forward. "Sounds intriguing."

Mary came straight to the point. "It's a long shot, but I'd like to rule out that there's a body buried in a spot next to the Community Garden."

"What? A body!" Alex said. "Have you notified the police?"

Mary chewed on her thumbnail. "Unofficially, yes. But I don't have enough evidence to get them involved. I was wondering, and I know it's a big ask, but would you two and your son be willing to go on a night dig for a few hours this Sunday?"

Sam leaned forward. Alex brought her hands to her face. They gazed at each other as if they communicated telepathically.

Alex spoke first as she shook their head. "I don't think so, Mary. We'd like to help you out, but—"

"We need to talk about this ourselves. Can we get back to you tomorrow?" Sam interrupted.

"Oh, sure." Mary had a sheepish grin.

I was too abrupt as usual. Who else could I call to help if they say no? Certainly not Ned.

"Dare we ask whose body you're looking for?" Alex asked.

"The less you know, the better, I think. Thanks for thinking about it. I look forward to hearing from you. Oh, by the way, this is on the QT. Ned wouldn't want me doing this." With that, Mary left.

Chapter 14

February 16, 2024

Having not heard from Alex by five on this Friday evening, Mary resolved she would have to do the Big Dig on her own. At least, she figured Blake could water down the area and rototill it for her ahead of time so the ground would be soft.

At five-thirty, a text from Alex arrived.

Alex: We talked it over. We're in as long as what we're doing isn't illegal. Our son even wants to recruit his friend. They're both nineteen. They live for this cloak-and-dagger sort of stuff.

Mary: Great! Not illegal, just not explicitly authorized. I'll take full responsibility.

Alex: OK.

Mary: Sunday night 10-1. Meet at the Garden. I'll bring supplies. Thanks!!!

Chapter 15

February 17, 2024

O n Saturday morning, Mary called Magnus to update him on her plan. They agreed the Big Dig was a long shot but saw little harm in trying. Magnus pointed out that even if Cora stole the will, the chances of finding it were remote because she would have destroyed it.

Undeterred, Mary said, "Oh, Magnus. One problem at a time, okay?"

"Good luck with the dig, Sis. Let those young, strong boys do most of the work."

"Sure thing. Bye."

* * *

Later that morning, Mary couldn't help noticing Ned's sullen mood. To lift his spirits, she suggested they take Chompers and walk to the library. Ned agreed, and they set off.

"You're doing a great job with Chompers. I'm grateful."

"Yeah, we get along okay."

"All right. What's wrong? What have I done?"

"You're so distracted, your work, the will, on the phone, and texting all the time. I feel ignored."

"You have your new friend here." Mary pointed at Chompers. "And your pickleball. You need to find more amusement, that's all. Let's pick up some DVDs for tonight, okay?"

"When are you going to retire? I want more of you."

"I have a few projects I want to finish up. You know I truly love my job. It will be hard for me to step away." Mary believed it would take more than a walk and a movie to lift Ned's spirits, so she devised another idea.

"Hey, it's nice out. We're supposed to hit the high fifties today and no rain. How about after the library, and we go out on the lake and row around for an hour?"

"We'd like that."

"Oh, you mean with Chompers?"

"Of course!"

* * *

The Colemans rented a small rowboat on the lake, as they had several times before. They weren't adequately prepared for the new element: Chompers. At first, the young dog resembled a whirling dervish as he surveyed his environment. After settling Chompers, they took in the scenery of lovely homes, evergreen firs dotting the hills surrounding the lake, and, best of all, a peek of majestic Mt. Hood covered with snow like meringue on a lemon pie.

Mary handed Ned sunscreen from the kangaroo pocket of her hoodie.

"Really, do I have to do this in February?" Ned asked.

"Yep. The sun's out. Come on. It's no big deal." Mary rubbed the lotion on her face and the back of her neck.

"Okay. You're probably right." Ned opened the tube and applied the SPF 30 to his face and hands.

They enjoyed their lake diversion until a gaggle of Canada geese decided to land in the water near their boat. Chompers barked like a cuckoo clock stuck on midnight, with his tail fiercely wagging. The dog, unable to resist, chased the birds into the water. He succeeded in scaring them off, but then Chompers didn't know what to do. He furiously swam in circles around the boat as Ned and Mary frantically called out his name. Eventually, he got close enough for Ned to grab his collar and pull him aboard.

"Thank goodness, Ned!"

"Yes, but I'm soaked."

"Yes, you are." Mary laughed. Chompers shook wholeheartedly, not once but twice, getting Mary almost as soaked as Ned.

They rowed back to the dock and turned in the boat. The three wet rats made their way back home. After showering and turning on the fireplace, they settled down to eat dinner and watch their favorite movie, *Moonstruck*. They recited several lines together out loud.

Chapter 16

February 18, 2024

O n Sunday afternoon, Mary found Ned at Denise's, accessing her monetary records to compile financial statements for 2023, keeping in mind tax filings. He told Mary how delighted Chompers behaved back in his home with Denise's scent still fresh on his sophisticated dog nose. Not finding her, he settled into his former spot beside Denise's desk. Mary told Ned she had errands to run.

Mary drove to the Parks supply warehouse and filled her Jeep Wagoneer with all the needed supplies. When she got home, she parked in the driveway, so when she left for the Big Dig that night, the garage door wouldn't wake Ned and Chompers. She moved all the work clothes she needed into the garage: jeans, boots, gloves, a warm hat, and a parka. She supplied the Jeep with water, candy bars, and chips.

Mary was relieved when Ned and Chompers went to bed at nine. She left a note on the counter in case Ned awoke:

Ned,
  I'm on a secret will mission.
  Don't worry.
  Love, Mary

At 9:20, Mary changed into her work clothes and left for the Community Garden. She needed to get there early to set up the lights for the crew. Earlier, she'd asked Blake to dampen the soil to make their job easier.

By 9:55, everyone had arrived, and Mary had cordoned off a ten-by-ten-foot area. "First, thanks everyone for coming. I know this is a long shot, but I appreciate your help. It's for a good cause to possibly uncover two crimes."

Mary tapped her chin. "I should add that there are potential risks. If we get caught, I'll take the blame. Most likely, we'll find nothing and not get caught. Best case, we'll find a body …"

At the word "body," the heads of the two young swiveled toward each other as if controlled by the same string. They met each other's gaze, and their mouths dropped.

"… and if we do, everyone can go home, and I'll call the police," Mary said. "Are you ready to start?"

"You bet," one teenager said.

"Yes," Sam said.

Heads nodded.

"Take rests when you need to. Water and snacks are in the back of the Jeep. Our goal is to dig two feet down over this area. The premise is that the grave is shallow. Ready? Let's dig!"

The group demonstrated enthusiasm at first. Mary encouraged the young men to pace themselves. The teens and Sam were the strongest and dug the most soil. Alex preferred baking to gardening and wasn't as outdoorsy as Sam, but she helped dig nonetheless.

By eleven-thirty, the group's activity flagged. With hands on their hips, most congregated near the snacks.

Sam and Alex's son kept digging, then said, "I hit something!"

"Nope, just a rock, Son," Sam said. "Basalt rock is the bane of every Pacific Northwest gardener."

Right before midnight, the tip of Sam's shovel hit something rubbery. The group moved in close to her area and dug like a dog searching for a bone. Mary focused her high-lumen flashlight on the spot.

"It looks like a shoe or a boot," Mary said as her heart pounded.

"Really?" Alex asked.

Eyes widened and bodies stiffened as everyone moved in closer to confirm the finding.

Mary felt a surge flow through her body as the hairs on her arm moved like wind on a field of grass.

"Whoa ..." one of the young men said, followed by a full body twirl. The other teenager performed a fist pump.

Alex said, "Wow, I never believed we'd find anything."

"Gently now. Let's expose what we think is a boot," Mary said. "Just Sam. All others, please shine your flashlights so she can see what she's doing." A Merrill hiking boot became apparent.

"Water!" Sam shouted.

Alex got her vibe and hustled to the SUV and retrieved several water bottles. They opened one up and glanced at Sam, who nodded. Then Alex poured water on the boot to wash away the mud. The group stood silently and watched.

"Look, we have to make sure this isn't just a buried shoe. Is there a foot attached? Determine that, and we're done," Mary said.

"Let's not expose any more than we have to," Alex said. "It could be really gross." She wrung her hands.

"I see a sock!" Sam yelled. "More water."

Alex obliged.

"Uh-oh," one of the young men said. "Police." A police car approached with the red and blue lights flashing.

"Everybody, stop. Put down your shovels. Our work is done. It's out of our hands now. I'll do the talking. Thank you, everyone, so much," Mary said. "Let's all gather near the Jeep and act casual."

Although Mary projected calm, her body trembled.

Alex's brows furrowed. "Sam?"

"It's okay, Alex." Sam reached for Alex's arm to reassure her. "It'll be fine."

The young men seemed detached, like actors in a TV drama.

The lights from the police car blinded everyone. Two officers emerged. Thankfully, one of them was Officer Joe.

"Mary?"

"Yes, Joe." Even though it was Joe, Mary's body shook.

"Meet Officer Jenkins. This is Mary Coleman from the Parks Department." They both walked toward Mary.

"Hello, Mary," Jenkins said.

Joe towered over the short, stocky woman. The tight ponytail pulled her hair against her skull, likely giving her a permanent headache.

"Officer," Mary replied curtly.

"What's going on, Mary?" Joe wore a stern expression.

By now, the three were in proximity, with the rest of the group behind Mary.

"We think we found something, Joe. May I show you?" Mary walked over to their dig site and used her flashlight to reveal the boot and sock.

"I'll be damned. Hoo boy. Looks like we have a murder investigation on our hands. You agree, Officer Jenkins?"

"Yes, sir, I do." The stoic officer enlivened as her eyes darted back and forth.

"If you would, Officer Jenkins, we'll need police tape around this area. We'll need a barrier to close the Community Garden and an officer to ensure no one enters. Call for backup." Turning to the Big Dig crew, he said, "And you all, I need your names now, and then we're going to make a trip down to the station to get your statements."

"I got you the evidence, Joe," Mary said.

Joe pursed his lips. "Yes, you did, Mary. Yes, you did."

* * *

Making statements at the police station took hours, even though their stories matched up. In the predawn hours, the police released them and drove them back to the Community Garden to retrieve their cars. Vehicles with flashing lights from multiple jurisdictions filled the parking area and beyond.

In Joe's vehicle, Mary asked, "What happens next, Joe?"

"It'll take time to identify the body."

"What about Cora? She's coming to my home for housecleaning at one o'clock."

Joe rubbed his chin. "Ahh ... This is tricky. You and I may have our suspicions, but we don't have any proof yet. If she is involved, we don't want her to find out about the body at the Community Garden. I'll try to drop by her home this morning."

"Let me know what you can when you can. Your priority is the body, of course. Mine is the will. Thanks. Sorry for all the late-night work tonight."

"Part of the job. You're way too involved in this investigation, Mary." Joe's eyes narrowed. "Look, you need to back off and let us do our work and take the time we need, okay?"

"Yes, Joe."

"I'll be in touch."

Chapter 17

After thanking her fellow Big Dig helpers, Mary headed home. She hadn't received a text from Ned, so she figured he was still asleep. As she walked in, Ned was reading the note she'd left on the kitchen counter.

"What's going on, Mary?" Ned scowled.

"Lots. Let's get some coffee, and I'll explain everything."

"Look at you. You're all muddy." Chompers sniffed her up and down.

Mary looked down at her clothes and agreed. "Right. Let me jump in the shower for a quick rinse off."

Ned stood with his arms akimbo. "Yeah, you do that. I don't know if I'm more mad or hurt. You think about that in the shower."

Mary skulked off.

After her shower, Mary joined Ned at the kitchen table. Wagging his tail, Chompers approached Mary, and she petted him. Mary glanced at the clock. She debated without deciding whether she would work today after being up all night. Explaining everything to Ned would also take time, but first she needed to address his feelings.

Mary reached across the table to hold Ned's hands. "I'm sorry, hon, truly. I feared you'd try and stop me. Wait till you hear what I have to say."

Ned tilted his head.

"I suspect Cora took the will to prevent the Community Garden from getting money for the expansion."

"That doesn't make sense. Why?" Ned asked, eyes narrowing.

"Last night, we found her husband's body buried near her Garden plot."

"What?" Ned placed the heels of his hands on his temples.

Mary's cell buzzed with an incoming call. Her boss's name, Victor, the city manager, appeared on her phone.

"This is Mary. That's correct, sir. Yes. I understand. Yes, sir. You'll tell my staff. Uh-huh. Thanks for calling.

"Well, that makes my decision about going to work easy." Mary pulled her lips to one side of her face. "They've suspended me for using Parks' equipment without authorization on city property with non-city employees. Victor is unhappy that the police got involved, bringing adverse publicity to the city."

"You don't seem too worried," Ned said.

"I don't think I've processed everything yet. I'm so tired." Mary dropped her head upon her folded arms on the table.

They moved to the family room and continued their marathon discussion. On the north side of the house, the room was dark and chilly. Mary left the light off and wrapped herself with a comforter. They sat side by side on the sofa.

Mary updated Ned, and she answered his many questions. He complained about Mary's involvement in the Big Dig.

"Most of all, I'm so hurt you didn't trust me enough to tell me about your operation," Ned said.

"I know. I'm sorry, hon. I knew how much you disapproved of it all, but I couldn't get the police to move forward. Can we talk more later? I'm dead tired. Pardon the pun."

"Not funny. I'm going to take Chompers for a walk. Hey, boy. Walk time!" Chompers wagged his tail and put his paws on Ned's knees. "This conversation is not over."

"Right. You two walk. I'm going to get some sleep." Mary retreated to their bedroom.

* * *

Mary woke to the sound of the doorbell. She looked at the clock on her nightstand. 12:58 p.m. Her heart raced. *Cora. Am I capable of acting naturally with her at a time like this?*

"Hi, Cora," Mary said as she opened the door.

"Hi, Mary. You're home. Are you sick?" Cora paused at the door.

Mary's heart quickened its pace. "Uh, you didn't happen to see Officer Joe this morning, did you?"

"No, why?"

Drowsy from her nap, Mary realized this was a stupid question she shouldn't have raised. She conjured up a lie.

"No reason. I ran into Joe recently, and I thought he had more questions about Denise. Never—"

Before Mary could get out the words, she spotted Joe parking his car in front of their driveway, blocking Cora's Honda Element.

Mary breathed in deeply. "Speak of the devil."

Cora put down her cleaning caddy and looked at Mary with her eyebrows scrunched up. They both waited as Joe came to the door.

"Hi, Joe," Mary said.

"Mary. Cora." To Cora, he said, "I'm hoping to ask you some more questions. Would you mind coming down to the station?"

"Can it be later? I'm working here. This is how I make my living," Cora whined.

"No worries, Cora." Mary rushed around, found her purse, and wrote out a check. "You've been through a lot. Here's a check for today, and I'll see you next week. Okay?" Mary handed the check to Cora to eliminate her objection.

"I'll move my car, Cora. Please follow me to the station."

Joe gave Mary a look before walking toward his car. It reminded her of her dad's expression before he delivered punishment.

After Joe and Cora left, Mary paced the living room as she bit the inside of her check. *Did Cora kill Floyd? What will happen to her? Did she take the will?* Mary lowered her head, placed her hands on her forehead, and groaned.

She wondered where Ned and Chompers were and spotted a note on the counter saying they were out doing errands. Mary unclenched her jaw. She grabbed Denise's house key and went next door, not knowing precisely what she'd do there. Although needed, cleaning out the refrigerator wasn't on the top of the list.

Having spent little time in the garage, Mary poked around in there. White melamine closets lined the walls, and she opened them up. She read labels with Denise's handwriting on boxes and bins on the shelves: *Christmas*, *wreaths*, *deck lighting*, *Goodwill*, and such. Then she spotted a pretty black box on the top shelf.

Mary found a stepladder nearby, climbed it, reached for

the box, and brought it down. She popped open the lid and discovered dozens of letters addressed to Denise going back years. They all had Peter's return address.

Love letters, perhaps?

Mary took the black box home and stashed it in their spare bedroom. For now, she didn't need to invade their privacy.

Chapter 18

February 20, 2024

For Mary, her day away from work passed slowly. She concentrated on self-care. Her day included exercising, napping, and scheduling her counseling appointments. Boredom led her to organize crowded cupboards. She tried rereading her favorite novel, *To Kill a Mockingbird*, but couldn't concentrate. Her cell came with her everywhere, even in the home, as she waited for Joe to call, and at last, he did.

"Hi, Joe." She held her breath, waiting for him to speak.

"Hi, Mary. I have some news. Not good, I'm afraid."

"Okay. Hit me with it." Mary exhaled.

"I probably shouldn't be telling you this. We interviewed Cora, and she confessed to killing her husband."

"Oh, my God." Mary knew this was a possibility, but the reality of it buckled her knees, and she grabbed the kitchen counter for support.

"There may be mitigating factors. Self-defense. Cora and her attorney have to work that out with the DA."

Mary's mind spun, and she doubted she had absorbed all of

Joe's words. "Oh. Poor Cora." *Would it be too self-serving to bring up the will? Yes, but I'm going to do it anyway.* "Were you able to find out anything about the will?"

"Yes, that came up. She destroyed it."

Mary gasped. Her gut lurched with the implications. She marched around the kitchen, and Chompers followed her, thinking it was a game.

"She believes the will was a copy."

"What? What makes her say that?" Mary stopped walking.

Joe paused, then stuttered, "Well, uh, she had looked in the will folder before and knew two copies existed."

"Right. The original and a copy. Denise showed me once."

"On the day Cora drummed up the courage to take the will, only one remained."

Mary wanted to jump out of her skin. She wished Joe would speak faster.

"Yes ..." Mary said, urging him on.

"When Cora got home, she reviewed the will, which confirmed the Community Garden was getting a large percentage of the estate. When she got to the signature page ..."

Joe's radio cracked and Mary heard voices, pausing his explanation.

"... Cora thought the signatures appeared dim. So she dampened her finger to see if they'd smear," Joe said. "They didn't, so she figured the will was a copy, not the original."

"I hope, I hope it was only a copy." Mary's teeth clenched. *The original may still exist.*

"I don't know where this leaves me. I need time to think on this. You know I'm on unpaid leave?"

"Yes. Word's gotten around."

"I want to defend what I did to keep my job."

"It's a tough situation." Joe cleared his throat.

Mary leaned against the kitchen wall. "Should I talk to the press to tell my side?"

"I don't know, Mary. That's outside my wheelhouse. You're already in hot water. If you want my advice, if you talk to the press, do it 'on background,' so they don't quote you."

Mary heard muffled voices and Joe saying he'd be right with them. "Sure. Good idea. Thanks for letting me know all this. I sure appreciate it, Joe."

"You're welcome. Chin up, Mary."

"Oh, before you hang up, should I reach out to Cora? I'm not sure—"

"I don't recommend it. You might get called as a witness if there's a trial."

"Oh, yeah. I didn't think of that. Okay, thanks. Bye."

Mary placed her phone on the kitchen table as a headache seized her.

Cora killed her husband.

She never had the original will.

The gravity of it all erupted inside her. She slammed her hands on the kitchen table and the self-inflicted pain hurt. Then she balled her hands into fists and released a muffled scream.

Ned came running from the back bedroom. "Mary? Are you okay?"

"No. I'm right back where I started. Nowhere."

Chapter 19

February 21, 2024

A s it turned out, Mary didn't need to worry about contacting the press because they called her when they got their hands on the police report. She took Joe's advice and talked off the record to the *Lake Waluga Gazette* and *The Oregon Chronicle*. She mentioned she was on unpaid leave, knowing they would confirm that with the city manager.

Mary debated how much to say about the missing will. Planning the Big Dig made little sense without revealing the impetus. Mary knew the press would continue contacting her if she wasn't transparent. With time running out, she disclosed the stakes: finding the original will would support local charities. She withheld which nonprofits would benefit and why it personally meant so much to her.

Chapter 20

February 22, 2024

After taking Chompers for his morning constitutional, Ned brought in the newspapers. The headlines read:

Lake Waluga Gazette: "Locals Find Buried Body Near Community Garden"

The Oregon Chronicle: "Lake Walugan Citizens Discover Buried Body"

Over coffee and bagels at their kitchen table, Mary and Ned pored over the articles.

"Well, how'd they do? Did they get it mostly right?" Ned asked. His eyes peered at Mary over his reading glasses.

"They did. Fortunately, they both mentioned that I'm on unpaid leave."

"Are you hoping these articles will get you reinstated because this could be an opportunity here?"

Mary crossed her arms, but she resisted a snort of derision.

"This isn't a good time to bring that up. You know I want to shepherd the Garden expansion. I'd like to leave the department on a high note."

"Yes, dear." The newspaper crinkled as Ned pulled it up to cover his face.

"Too bad the papers mentioned Sam, Alex, and the boys. I hope they won't suffer for that."

Ned lowered his glasses on his nose and looked straight at Mary. "You kidding? The community will treat them as heroes."

"Hope so."

As they cleaned up the morning dishes, their conversation moved to Cora.

"I still can't believe that Cora killed her husband. The woman has been in our home every week for ten years. How can we know her so little? That's on us, isn't it, dear?" Ned asked as he dried his hands on the tea towel.

"Partly. Well, Cora hid her true self. Embarrassment. Shame. But I agree. We need to do better." Mary refilled her coffee cup. She glanced out the window to see a goldfinch land on the thistle bag. The bird turned upside down and pecked.

Ned gathered the papers and moved to the sofa. Chompers lay dozing on his bed nearby. "I've been waiting to fill you in on Denise's finances. Are you open to hearing about that?"

"Sure. I appreciate you doing that. I'm discouraged that I may not have any power to fulfill Denise's wishes. It infuriates me that Wayne may get it all. Do you think I should hire an attorney?"

"Let's talk about one thing at a time. I've determined that Denise's estate is worth nearly three million dollars."

"Really?" Mary's jaw went slack.

"Besides the value of her home, did you know that Denise owns the adjacent vacant lot?"

"No way! She never mentioned that."

"The property tax bill revealed that. Denise didn't spell out that the lot goes to Peter, so my take is that its value gets rolled into the other assets like cash, CDs, her car, life insurance, etc. All that could go to the charities. But you're the executor."

"Personal representative, actually. No loans, then?"

"Nope."

"We'll see." Mary forced a smile.

"Now, getting back to the attorney question. Denise's estate could pay for an attorney, but only if you win in court. A court case can get very expensive. And if we lose, and Wayne gets everything, I suspect we'd be personally out the attorneys' fees, which could be substantial."

"I can't think about this anymore today. I need a break. Shall we take Chompers for a walk?"

"Good idea. Sure." He turned to Chompers. "Are you up for that, boy?"

Chompers heard the *W* word and was already standing by the door, wagging his tail.

The three of them strolled through their neighborhood, lined with trees. Despite the cherry and apple trees being bare, the Douglas firs provided greenery. Orange-tinged pine needles covered the ground beneath holly bushes dotted with red berries.

"Ned! It's a cedar waxwing with a holly berry in its mouth," Mary said.

Ned didn't turn around. His body pointed toward their house. "Oh, no," he said.

Mary followed Ned's glance and saw what he was looking at—Wayne, sitting on his motorcycle in Denise's driveway.

"Oh, crap. I don't need this."

As Chompers pulled on the leash when he realized their proximity to home, Ned said, "We'll be civil and then go inside. It'll be fine."

Wayne got down on his haunches and held his arms to the approaching Chompers. "Hey, boy!" He gently petted the dog and spoke in a chipper manner. Chompers's tail revealed his delight.

Ned said, "Hello, Wayne."

"Ned, Mary. Is this Denise's dog, Chompers?"

"Yes," Mary said in a clipped tone. She wondered how he knew that. *Maybe he was in town for Thanksgiving.*

"Hey, Chompers. Good boy. You remind me of my dog during incarceration." Wayne stood up. "We had a program called Pup Redux, where we trained rescue dogs. It made the time there bearable. I got very attached to mine."

"We support a similar program. What brings you by?" Ned asked.

Turning to Mary, he said, "So you know, I'm in town till the end of the month. That's all." He got on his motorcycle, put on his helmet, and started the engine.

"Okay," Mary said.

"See ya around, guys. Bye, pooch." And he was off.

"Have we been too hard on him, dear?" Ned asked.

"I don't know. Officer Joe once mentioned he thought Wayne was smart and needed a strong male figure to turn him in the right direction. But people make choices, don't they?"

"Yeah, they do. The dog likes him."

"Chompers loves everyone," Mary said.

Chapter 21

February 23, 2024

Mary couldn't sleep and arose early. She went through the motions of making coffee and cooking her frozen waffle in the toaster oven. When she glanced at the wall calendar, the date took her aback. *Is it Friday the 23rd already?* She dropped her head on her chest.

Mary had already decided she couldn't ask Ned to risk their savings to hire an attorney to fight the will in court. After breakfast, she desired a shower to lift her spirits. En route, her intuition kicked in, leading her to pause in front of the guest room. She spotted the black box containing the letters between Peter and Denise.

Those may be my last leads to follow.

By the time Mary got out of the shower, she had her game plan figured out. She turned the guest room into a staging area for all the letters. Mary sorted them into reverse chronological order. They dated back to 2000, starting twenty-four years ago.

In 2001, Peter sent a first-anniversary card:

My love for you knows no bounds. It was the best day of my life when you entered my computer class. My attraction to you was immediate. I'm the luckiest guy in the world.

So that's how they met. At the Lake Waluga Community Center for a computer training class. He's rather corny, but sweet.

In 2004, Peter urged Denise to marry him:

I know you think there's too big a difference in our ages, but I don't care! We've been together for four years. Trust that. Marry me, my love.

He truly cares for her. This nerdy guy is rather romantic.

Two years later, Peter revealed Microsoft was interested in his computer app:

This will be a dream come true, Denise. If MS buys my app, I'll be set for life!

By consulting Google and Magnus's background report, Mary confirmed when Peter became a tech millionaire. It was difficult to determine how much wealth he gained because it involved stock shares. Three years later, Peter bought the Lake Waluga house and the vacant lot next door for Denise.

In 2009, Peter wrote:

It brings me so much joy to give you the house. I know you always wanted to live in the Lakeview neighborhood,

but couldn't afford it. I have more money than I know
what to do with. You being happy makes me happy.

So that's why Denise willed Peter the house! She was returning the
gift.

Their relationship cooled for a few years. By 2011, according
to Magnus's background check, Peter married Kimberly. Mary
found their wedding photo online.

The letters stopped for a while, and then, in 2014, the relationship heated up again:

> *You're the one. You were always the one. I only married*
> *Kimberly because you wouldn't marry me, and I needed*
> *someone for my career. That's an awful thing to say, I*
> *know. Thank you for being back in my life. It may sound*
> *trite, but you complete me.*

Taken right from the movie screen.

The letters tapered off then, and Mary concluded they had
changed to WhatsApp, a secure application she had heard of but
never used.

Peter's emotional outbursts make me think the relationship was
ongoing ...

* * *

Mary's therapist suggested she get more exercise without
distractions. Heeding that advice, Mary drove to Waluga Farm
without Ned, Chompers, or even her phone. The weather
was cloudy and mild for February. Mary concentrated on her
breathing and steps to be mindful of her actions as a form of

meditation. She paused when she reached the labyrinth. *Oh, yeah, I'm supposed to choose a particular problem and then stroll through the labyrinth to solve it.*

Mary focused on Peter and his potential role in the missing will. After all, he was her last hope because he had a long relationship with Denise and frequently visited her home. At first, she didn't believe the labyrinth was working. Eventually, warmth and serenity settled in as the sun appeared. Mary proceeded slowly and deliberately on the path.

Mary's history with Peter came to her in images: his VW van in Denise's driveway monthly through the years, how hard he took the news of Denise's death, and his sobbing at the memorial service and his familiarity with Denise's home. Then she remembered the password he tried. From their letters, she knew 2000 in Chompers2000! was the year they'd met. And how he froze when he saw the electronic will revealing he was getting the house.

When Mary reached the labyrinth's center, she raised her arms in exultation as she saluted the sun shining on her. She knew what she would do next.

* * *

Back at home, Mary took out her cell, sat on the family room sofa, and dialed Joe.

"Hi, Joe. Can I buy you lunch?" Mary asked. "I want to make up for all the trouble I caused."

"You don't need to do that. It's part of the job."

"Look, in all honesty, I want to run something past you." Mary tapped her pen on the kitchen table like a woodpecker on a tree trunk.

"Always an agenda with you, Mary. Lucky for you, I'm hungry, and I enjoy your company."

"The diner on Main Street? Whatever time works for you."

"One o'clock. See you then," said Joe.

* * *

As Mary walked into the Lake Diner, she breathed deeply to enjoy the smells of fried onions and truffle fries. In the back, she spotted a free booth and sat down to wait for Joe. She loved this diner, the red leather stools, the comfy private booths, and their award-winning curly fries. She lingered over the vintage photos from the '60s of young women on water skis forming human pyramids on the lake.

As Mary sipped her Cherry Coke, Officer Joe came in. He waved at a few patrons and at the waitress behind the counter. Everyone liked Joe, despite his authoritative presence. Mary brought him up to speed with the facts that led her to her latest theory.

"Bottom line, I think Peter is a needy guy emotionally. Losing Denise devastated him. He doesn't need money."

"I'm starting to think you have a new suspect," Joe said, then sipped his Coke.

"I have proof, letters showing their longtime relationship."

"So?" Despite his objection, Joe revealed his dimples.

"You want a motive, don't you? Well, here it is. Denise was going to bequeath Peter the house."

"How is that a problem?"

Ignoring Joe's snark, Mary said, "Peter's married. How would he explain that? It would reveal their affair."

"Okay, I'm seeing that."

His slight nod gave Mary encouragement. "I think he took the will." Mary's look intensified.

"I'd be hard-pressed to doubt you, Mary, after you solved an unknown murder in this town. How do you expect him to reveal his alleged theft?" Joe shrugged one shoulder.

"Well, I have a plan."

"Of course you do. And it involves me, doesn't it?" Joe tipped his head and sighed.

The waitress approached and took their order. Joe ordered a BLT, curly fries, and a chocolate shake.

Mary ordered a grilled cheese and curly fries with an extra dill pickle. *Is the waitress actually batting her eyes at Joe?* Mary stifled a giggle, although she couldn't deny the attraction.

"By the way, I have to pay for my meal. Regulations," Joe said.

"Sure. My plan is to ask Peter over to Denise's because there's one more password I can't figure out. That's my ruse. When he comes over, I'll confront him. Then, you drop by to increase the pressure. That's it. That's my plan." Mary extended her arms as if to say, *Voilà!*

Mary put her elbows on the table and her chin on her hands. "Let me remind you that Denise's will, if found, would donate hundreds of thousands to wonderful causes."

Joe shifted in his seat. "And how exactly do I come in?"

"I see you as adding intensity for Peter to do the right thing. I'm unsure if you should be there ahead of time or come after I confront him as if you're doing a drive-by or something. If you're game, let's brainstorm."

"This is a big ask, Mary." Joe's head shook slightly. "I've got rules to follow, time to account for, and superiors to report to."

"Come on, let's put our heads together. We can figure this out." Mary winked at Joe.

Joe breathed deeply and released a long sigh. He stoked his chin. Moments passed, and then he forced a smile.

Chapter 22

N ed insisted on accompanying Mary to confront Peter before Officer Joe arrived. Ned suggested a soft approach.

Mary's stomach roiled as Peter's van coasted up Denise's driveway. He had turned the engine off on the street, an old habit she had observed through the years. Ned was fooling around with the fireplace to make the room warm and cozy and to appear nonchalant. Peter knocked, and Mary opened the door.

"Thanks for coming, Peter."

He wore a Portland Blazers cap, and his longish hair poked out above his ears. "Sure, Mary." Peter immediately noticed Ned and lifted his hand in a casual wave.

Mary introduced the two, and they shook hands.

"So you need help with the QuickBooks password?" Peter asked.

"Actually, no. Can we talk?" Mary tried to sound easygoing, but her nerves showed when her voice quavered.

Peter took a step back, and his body stiffened. "About what?"

"Let's sit." Mary sat on the sofa and pointed Peter toward the chair.

Ned stoked the fire some more, even though it didn't need it.

"I still haven't found the will, Peter. You remember all the good charities designated to get Denise's estate?" She picked up Denise's pie chart and held it up for him to see. "Kids, the homeless, the hungry, and the Community Garden. If I can't find the will, Denise's greedy in-and-out-of-trouble nephew will get everything. We don't want that."

Peter shook his head as he listened. The room beheld the tension of one shoe having dropped, with another sure to follow.

"Would inheriting the house be a problem for you? With your wife, I mean? I found your letters, so I know you've been involved with Denise for a long time."

"You read my letters?" Peter stood up and raised his arms in the air. His thin build and long arms made him appear taller than he already was.

Ned walked over to be near Mary.

"Look, Peter. Do you know anything about the original will?" Mary took hold of Ned's arm, not addressing Peter's question. "I understand you don't want to create a problem between you and your wife." As Mary said the words, she heard a car door slam. Joe had arrived.

Peter's face turned crimson. "You keep my wife out of this. I have been helpful to you in every way, and this is how you thank me? By accusing me? I don't—" His booming voice echoed.

Joe's knock interrupted him.

Mary went to the door. "Hi, Joe. Come on in."

Joe surveyed the room. He removed his wet hat and observed scowling faces. Bodies stood still.

"Hi, everyone. How's it going?" Joe's ambled into the room, calming the mood down.

"Pretty tense, Joe," Ned said. The wind splattered rain on the front window.

Peter headed to the door. "I'm leaving."

"I'll need to move my car first. I'm Joe, by the way. Peter, is it? Why don't we just sit down for a minute?"

"Nope. No way." Peter's head shook back and forth like windshield wipers. To Joe he said, "I need you to move your car now."

Joe flipped his palms over and shrugged his shoulders as he glanced at Mary.

Peter acted jittery and gasped short, rapid breaths.

"Can someone catch me up?" Joe asked.

"I've hinted that Peter had a good reason for taking the will," Mary said.

"I see. Well, let me be more explicit. Did you take the will, Peter?" Joe asked in an even-toned voice.

Peter's arms extended, mimicking a porcupine's protruded quills when under threat. "Is this an interrogation? Do I need a lawyer?"

Joe turned to Mary. "I think you have your answer, Mary. I better let him go." Joe opened the door, went outside, moved his car, and drove away.

Peter followed him and then sped off.

Mary and Ned found themselves alone in Denise's house.

"Now what do I do?" Mary tapped her fingers on her lips.

Chapter 23

February 25, 2024

O n Sunday morning, the day after the confrontation with Peter, Mary prepared their morning coffee. Ned and Chompers strolled in. As they ate their toast, Mary's with margarine and Ned's with peanut butter and jelly, they discussed the night before.

"I think Peter's got the will," Mary said. "If he didn't take it, I think the first words out of his mouth would have been 'no,' as in 'I didn't take the will.'"

"Could be. Or the accusation shocked him. Maybe his go-to response is 'call the lawyers' because he's rich, and that's what they do." Ned took a big bite.

He looked up at his wife over his reading glasses. "You know, dear ... I've been reluctant to bring this up, but if Peter took the will, why would he leave the electronic version on Denise's computer?"

Mary hung her head down. "I dunno. Maybe he forgot about it?"

Ned sighed.

"I feel so helpless. The end of the month is Thursday. Wayne will make another appearance at any time. I've done all I can, haven't I?" Mary pressed her lips together.

As Ned put more jelly on his toast, he said, "Yes, dear. You've gone above and beyond. You solved a murder, for goodness' sake."

"Yeah. I don't know what to do about Cora. Should I call her? Should I just let things be? She probably hates me. Don't answer me. I can't think about that situation right now. I'll bring it up with my therapist next week." She took a sip of her coffee.

"I thought Joe recommended against contacting Cora."

"He did. It's still on my mind. So unfinished, you know? I don't even know when I'm returning to work. I haven't heard from Victor. Hey, let's check out the papers for updates."

"I need to take Chompers out. I'll go grab the papers on my way back in." Ned leashed up the dog, put his coat over his robe and slippers, and went outside.

While they were out, Mary's phone buzzed with an incoming text.

Peter: Yesterday freaked me out. Can we meet again? Somewhere neutral. You and me.

Mary showed Ned the text when he and Chompers returned. As Mary thought about how to respond to Peter, Ned toweled off the dog.

Mary spread the newspapers out on the table, revealing the headline of the *Lake Waluga Gazette*: "Woman Arrested for Community Garden Murder." Mary read the story out loud. "I think it's a fair article, do you?"

"Uh-huh."

Mary flipped to the Letters to the Editor section. "Oh, Ned. Oh, my."

"What is it?" Ned stood up to read over her shoulder.

"The community. They're standing up for me." Mary's voice cracked. She read aloud the headings of three letters to the editor:

"Parks Director Did City a Favor"

"Coleman Saved City Money"

"Parks Director Punished for Solving a Crime?"

As she pored over the comments of her neighbors, friends, and people she didn't know, tears dampened her cheeks.

Ned hugged her from behind and whispered, "Of course, dear. People appreciate you in this town."

"Peter! I almost forgot about his text. I want nothing to spoil this day. I'll text him and agree to meet him at the Community Garden tomorrow."

"I'll be in the car monitoring you two."

"As you wish." Mary grinned at Ned.

* * *

Later on Sunday afternoon, the rain let up, and Mary walked into the neighborhood. She didn't want to hide in the house anymore. The letters from the community gave her resolve and confidence. As she strolled, she called Magnus to update him on everything.

"Do you feel safe meeting Peter?" Magnus asked.

"Oh, sure. I think he's harmless. He's a boy who's lost his love, also his mother figure, but I won't go there. I think he's scared and wants his cake and to eat it, too. Immense wealth will do that to a person."

"You need leverage to get him to come forward."

"Isn't the threat of police involvement and a possible felony enough leverage?"

"I don't think you can prove anything. Does Peter still have the will if he took it? You need more. Let's see ... Give me a sec." Magnus clicked his tongue.

The call went silent momentarily, and then Magnus cleared his throat. "Here are my thoughts. Remind him that the best way to love Denise now is to fulfill her wishes from the will."

Mary wished she were at home to write everything down, but she listened intently.

"Also, he needs insurance so he won't get in trouble with the law. The fact that you've brought in Officer Joe is kinda a dual-edged sword. It puts pressure on him to act but is scaring him, too."

"Right." She skirted around a small puddle as she walked.

"Plus, we think he's worried about his wife finding out about his affair. Is there some way you can assure him that won't get out?"

Mary picked up the pace toward home. "Good points, all. I've got some ideas, but I want to think this through. One solution would come at great personal cost to me."

"You mean telling him about your six-month break during college?"

"Thanks for the advice. I'll let you know how it goes."

Chapter 24

February 26, 2024

O n Monday at 11:50 a.m., Ned and Mary pulled up at the Community Garden parking lot. The car thermometer registered 38 degrees, and the sky drizzled.

"I'm going to get out to wait for him so he doesn't get spooked by your presence," Mary said.

"It's cold and sprinkling." Ned frowned.

"I've got my hooded coat," Mary said as she opened the car door.

"Wave your arms if you want me to come."

"I'm hoping that won't be necessary."

A little after noon, Peter arrived, not in his classic VW Van but in his late-model Tesla. He spotted Mary near the Community Garden office and joined her. As Peter approached, Mary pointed her finger toward a path so they could have more privacy. Together, they walked to a quiet spot.

"Can you do me a favor and shut off your phone?" Peter asked.

"Sure. Will you do the same?" They both turned off their cells.

"Look, Peter, all I want is for Denise's charities to get the money she intended."

"I know ..." He bowed his head.

"I'm sorry about bringing in Officer Joe, but I have only a couple of days before Denise's nephew asserts his rights with no will—and he gets everything. Denise wouldn't have wanted that." As Mary was speaking, she observed Blake milling about.

He waved at her, and she waved back.

Peter bounced up and down. "I know ... How can I be sure that if I give you the will, two things won't happen? My wife can never know about my long-standing affair with Denise, and I don't want any trouble with the police."

HE HAS THE WILL.

Mary took a big breath. "You have the original will, then?"

Peter nodded.

"When did you take it?"

"Late last year sometime. When she mentioned giving me the house again, despite my objections, I knew I had to do something."

Mary's emotions spun like liquid in a blender, a mix of hot anger and cool relief. She found her bearings and said, "I've thought about your risks. A lot. Your first request is simple. You can have your letters, and you'll have my silence on that. I'm not into breaking up people's marriages."

"Good. And my second request?" Peter warmed his hands by rubbing them together.

"Your second request ... Oh, boy, I can't believe I'm going to do this." Mary stared up at the sky and clasped her hands as if asking for heavenly strength.

"Do what?" Peter asked.

"I have a secret, a big secret I've never told anyone. My husband, who is lovingly looking out for me in the parking lot, doesn't even know this. If I tell you this, I don't want a soul in the world to know it. This gives you leverage to ensure I won't breathe a word about your infidelity and illegal act. Is that a deal?"

After Mary decided to reveal her truth, her stomach lurched as it did on a high-speed elevator.

"It better be a big secret."

"It is." *Can I do this?*

"Let's hear it." Peter shook his arms to get warm.

"Have you noticed that man working as we've been talking? He's pushing the wheelbarrow down that path now." Mary tilted her head in that direction.

"You mean that African American man?"

"Yes."

"What about him?"

"His name is Blake James. He's my son."

There. I said it. Strangely, her muscles relaxed.

"Why is it a secret? There's nothing to be ashamed of."

"Of course not. I'm exceedingly proud of Blake. But he doesn't know I'm his mother. He was the product of a one-night stand in 1984. It was a different world then, Peter. I was barely out of my teens and wasn't fit to be a parent."

Peter's body changed from rigid to soft, and he craned his neck in sympathy.

"So, I went away to my aunt's in Washington, had the baby, gave him up for adoption, and came home. It was a closed adoption. I didn't know who adopted him, and no one could discover who I was. That's what people did in those days." Mary stared at the ground.

"I have so many questions. Like, how did he come to be here at the Garden?"

"Serendipity. His nonprofit's application came across my desk, and it included his bio. We ran a background check as we do for all our subcontractors. I got an inkling that Blake could be my son, so I asked my brother, who's a PI, to do an extensive check. Once I witnessed the birth certificate, I knew. It had the exact date, time, and place, but without my name, of course."

"Why don't you tell him?" Peter stepped closer.

Mary scanned for Blake to ensure he couldn't hear them. "From speaking with Blake, I realized he doesn't know he's adopted." Mary flashed back to the moment he said he wasn't like either of his folks, which convinced her Blake thought they were his biological parents.

Mary's hands jutted out. "His parents withheld that truth. Can you imagine how huge a shock that would be? I don't want to upset his family or mine."

"It's none of my business, but why not share this with your husband?"

"You're right. It's not your business, but since you want to be assured of my secrecy, I'll say more."

Peter's eyes bore into Mary's.

"I learned the hard way, years ago. The only way to keep something a secret is to tell no one. Magnus knew about the pregnancy and adoption because he's my little brother and was around then, but he doesn't know that the baby was Blake."

Mary's hands came together as if in prayer. Peter nodded with rapt attention. "Knowing Ned as I do, he'd want me to tell Blake the truth, and for me, that's too big a risk of harm. So, what do you say, Peter?"

Peter strolled up and down the walkway a bit. With his hand extended, he walked back toward Mary and said the magic words: "You have a deal. I'll keep your secret, and you'll keep mine."

As Mary shook his hand, her face beamed. "Thank you, Peter."

"Do you have the will with you?"

"No. Can we meet at Denise's house at four o'clock tomorrow? I'll have it then," Peter said.

"By the way. Just curious. Why did you give me the password to Denise's computer and show me the will program?"

"Ah ... that." Peter rubbed his hands together. "Frankly, it didn't occur to me she did the will herself. I could tell I had the original. From novels I've read, I knew only original wills properly signed matter."

Mary pulled her coat closer to her body.

"Maybe it was naïve, but I didn't think you'd suspect me," Peter said.

"Well, it's cold and starting to rain harder. Tomorrow, then. You're doing the right thing, Peter."

Mary walked briskly back to the car and couldn't wait to tell Ned the news.

Chapter 25

Mary felt a surge of nervous energy the morning after learning Peter had the original will. She threw herself into cleaning the house from top to bottom. The house missed Cora. She tidied the guest room and then returned the black box containing Denise and Peter's correspondence to Denise's desk.

In the midafternoon, Mary, Ned, and Chompers went for a walk in the neighborhood. The day was cloudy and dim, but not raining. As they drew near home, Mary noticed lights on in Denise's house. Worse yet, smoke slithered out of the chimney.

"Oh, no!" Mary bolted toward Denise's house without explanation. She ran past Peter's VW van parked in the driveway. *What is burning? It better not be the will.*

She opened the front door and burst in. Peter fed his letters from the black box into the fireplace.

Mary was out of breath from running. "I didn't realize you had a key to Denise's."

"Oh, yeah. Since I bought it." He tossed another letter in.

"I'm a bit on edge until I get the will in my hands."

"Oh, I understand. I'll get it for you in a second. Here's the last letter." He placed it on the log, where it singed, curled, and evaporated into ash and smoke. Peter wiped the wetness from his eyes on his sleeve. "I'll get the will now."

With so much at stake, Mary still didn't trust Peter. He walked out to his van, and Mary followed him out. He pressed the button to open the back hatch and opened it. He pushed aside a few boxes and then opened the wheel well. A waterproof document holder lay atop the spare tire. Peter handed it to Mary. She opened it to see the familiar document. Quickly, she flipped to the last page to see Denise's signature and the two witnesses' signatures.

The will was in the van all this time.

"Thank you, Peter. I hope everything goes well with your wife."

"I'm sorry for all the trouble I caused you. I guess that's it."

"I'll be in touch when it comes time to turn the house over to you."

"Yep." Peter hopped into his van and started it up.

"So long, Peter." He gave a wave of the hand, and he was off.

Ned arrived at Denise's house, but he and Chompers had hung back to let them talk. When Peter left, Mary's broad smile and relaxed body revealed that all was well. Ned took Chompers home for his post-walk cookie.

Preoccupied, Mary walked into Denise's place and, warmed by the fireplace, sat on the sofa to read the will. It was identical to the electronic one, but had two surprises. First, the witnesses were her neighbors, Sam and Alex. Mary had never considered that. Second, Denise added a handwritten note in her lovely cursive writing on the last page.

Dear Mary,

Sorry you're left with this unpleasant duty of being my
executor. I hope it isn't too much trouble. You have my
eternal (get it?) gratitude. I have one more favor to ask.
Will you and Ned take Chompers for me? He's a handful,
but I have the feeling he's just what Ned needs to keep
busy in his retirement.

xo

Denise

Mary laughed at the "much trouble" remark. Then she cried.
She cried the tears of mourning she had held back for weeks.
She cried tears of relief.

Chapter 26

The morning after getting the original will, Mary and Ned had coffee and breakfast at their kitchen table. It was Wednesday, so Ned had newspapers to read. Chompers slept in his bed and wiggled his feet as if running in a dream.

"So, you're okay with keeping Chompers?"

Hearing his name, Chompers popped his head up.

"I'm more than okay with it. Denise bequeathed him to me. We're buddies now." Ned grinned.

Chompers's head lay back down, unbeknownst to the consequential moment.

"Did you hear the motorcycle driving by a few times last night?"

"Nope. I slept like a baby."

"What time are you going to file the will?"

"As soon as they open at nine this morning."

* * *

Mary called Ned from the Probate Department. "You're not going to believe this!"

"Is everything okay?" Ned asked.

"Yes, but remember how I said I Googled info about how much time I had to find the will?"

"Uh-huh. Thirty days."

"Right. And that got reinforced by Wayne's threats."

"Yes."

"I had four months! My Google search landed on the wrong page."

"How 'bout that. Well, you saved yourself three months of agony, right?"

"I guess. Oh, well. See you soon."

Chapter 27

February 29, 2024

On Leap Day, Mary got a phone call from her boss.

"This is Mary."

"Mary, this is Victor."

"Yes, sir."

"Good news. I've talked to the mayor and the city council. We've cleared you to come back to work. Can you start tomorrow?"

"Sure thing. And about my back pay?" Mary grimaced at her chutzpah.

"I can go over the details with you then, but suffice it to say that the community overwhelmingly feels you should be forgiven for accessing city property and using city tools without authorization. You'll receive back pay."

"That's wonderful, Victor."

"We'll need to add a formal reprimand to your personnel file, but there will be no consequences."

"Understood. See you tomorrow."

* * *

Later that day, Wayne pulled into their driveway and sat on his chopper. Ned and Chompers were on a walk. Mary came out to greet him.

"Wayne."

"Mary." He squinted at the sun in his eyes. "Well?"

"I found the will and filed it yesterday at the Probate Department. I need to let you know that you're not in it," Mary said.

"I'm sorry to hear that."

"Do you want a copy? Or I can tell you what's going where. Your aunt's estate mostly goes to charity, very good causes."

"I thought I was a good cause." Wayne's right eyebrow rose.

Mary kicked a fir tree twig near her feet. "You got a rough start to life. You've made some bad choices along the way. It's never too late to turn over a new leaf—"

Wayne started up his motorcycle, drowning out the rest of her sentence.

"Wait! Wayne, I have something to say. Will you hear me out?"

Wayne shut off the engine.

"We may never see each other again, so I want you to know that your aunt cared about you."

"Not enough to give me an inheritance."

"Well, no. Perhaps she worried you'd gamble it away. Another thing I wanted to tell you is that Officer Joe shared that he thinks you're very smart. That's something you could build from."

Wayne rolled the motorcycle back and forth.

"And one last thing. I know you have potential because you're good with Chompers. Anyway, I hope you'll make the most of your gifts."

Wayne slowly backed out of the driveway. He turned the engine on and gave Mary a flick of his hand as he drove away.

* * *

When Mary returned to her downtown office, her team stood and gave her an ovation. She addressed them.

"Thank you, one and all, for your patience and for covering for me during this last rough month. I'm so grateful to have you on my team and to be working with you. And now for some news. I have it on good authority that the Community Garden will be expanding. Stay tuned for more information."

They applauded, and Mary went into her office to make an important call.

* * *

"Blake here."

"Hi, Blake, it's Mary."

"Hi, how are you?"

"Well, thank you. I have some great news for you about the Community Garden ..."

Epilogue

Eighteen months later, the Community Garden hosted a groundbreaking celebration for its expansion. The sun shone brightly, and the crowd was cheerful. Everyone attended, even Magnus came up from California to celebrate his sister's perseverance and to reconnect with old friends.

Officer Joe explained to Mary that Cora was making a deal with the district attorney. She agreed to plead guilty to an affirmative defense and will serve six months of community service.

"Guess where, Mary?" Joe asked, his dimples showing.

"Tell me, Joe."

"The Community Garden."

They clinked cups of apple cider as they laughed at the irony.

But then Joe's face grew grave, and his eyebrows furrowed. "I want to say ... Cora had a difficult childhood, too. She's had a tough life and could use a friend."

"Leave that to me, Joe. Top priority. I'll be in touch with her soon," Mary said.

"I knew you would."

"Denise would want me to, as well."

They turned their attention to Blake, who spoke animatedly to a group about the expansion plans. He talked about more gardening beds, including an area for children, a building for various training classes, and an elaborate composting area and irrigation system.

Mary glimpsed Peter in the crowd, and he winked at her as Blake spoke. She nodded and couldn't help noticing his wife looked pregnant. After speaking with his attorneys, Peter had learned he could disclaim the house inheritance, which left more for the charities.

The Big Dig gang—Sam and Alex, their son, and his friend—attended the celebration. Although the hole they had dug had disappeared, the teenagers stood near the spot with their peers retelling their experience.

A slimmed-down Ned and the irrepressible Chompers joined Mary. He shared that he had signed the waiting list for a gardening plot. Mary smiled and grabbed his hand.

"You know, hon ..." Mary said.

"Yes, dear."

"I've decided to submit my retirement paperwork."

"You have? What are you going to do with all your free time?"

"Do you think I could join your pickleball group?"

"We always need subs. I bet you could worm your way into being a regular."

"I know what I won't be doing—signing up to be anyone's personal representative for their will ever again."

Ned chuckled. "This day must be gratifying, all your work coming to fruition."

"Well, none of this would have happened without Denise's vision and generosity."

"True, but if you hadn't persisted through enormous challenges ..."

"I'll give you that. I think I keep coming back to her pie

chart attached to her office wall. It's her legacy. Circumstances jeopardized it for a while, but now it's a reality. I sure miss her."

Mary glanced at Blake, beaming as he described the future of the Community Garden. She placed her hand on her heart and then looked up to the sky.

I may have helped secure your legacy, my friend, but you made my secret dream of seeing my son's vision come true. Thank you, dear one.

Note

Thank You for Reading!

The author hopes you enjoyed *Willful Obsession.* Your thoughts and feedback are incredibly valuable, and they also help other readers discover new books.

If you enjoyed this story, consider leaving an honest review on the platform where you purchased or downloaded the ebook (e.g., Amazon, Goodreads).

It only takes a moment, but it makes a world of difference!

Thank you again for your support.

Warm regards,

Star Ruby Publishing

About the Author

Kristy Schnabel grew up in Southern California, where she earned her business degrees. She has worked in the private, government, and entrepreneurial sectors.

Peak life experiences include being a Junior Lifeguard, SCUBA diving with a shark, and swimming from Washington to Oregon on the Columbia River. Her solo literary trips to London at ages 40 and 65 stand out as special travel experiences. She's a former synchronized swimmer and curler, and now is learning to play bridge. Fluency in Spanish eludes her, but she never stops trying.

As a lifelong learner, after retirement, Kristy returned to school and completed an English degree that had eluded her earlier. Then, she tried a creative writing course and caught the writing bug. Her short stories appeared in *Letter & Line* and *The Pointed Circle* literary magazines.

Kristy and her husband, Larry, live in Oregon.

You can connect with me on:

🌐 https://kristyschnabel.com

🔗 https://www.instagram.com/kkschnabel

🔗 https://www.youtube.com/@KristySchnabel

🔗 https://www.threads.com/@kkschnabel

Subscribe to my newsletter:

✉ https://kristyschnabel.com